THE
Seeker
OF
Nothing

A FABLE ON
OWNING YOUR LIFE

Kabir Munjal

First published in India in 2022

Copyright © Kabir Munjal 2022

ISBN: 978-93-5551-298-7

Om Swamiji, words cannot encapsulate what my heart knows. This book is yours. Thank you for being by my side every step of the way. Your grace and blessings make my life beautiful.

Mom, this would not be possible without you. Your thoughts, input, and support have been invaluable in making this a reality.

Dad, thank you for always being the father I needed.

Bee, I am grateful for your love and support. Thank you for standing by me.

Varun Jain, thank you so very much for your support and kindness. It has been extremely helpful.

A big thank you to everyone who helped me have the experiences I needed to make this happen.

Ned-Har

"Will you get off the ship tomorrow?"

I peer into Andahar's cabin and find him sitting at his shabby desk, trying to fix himself a pipe. With those trembling hands? He may be here until hell freezes over.

I use my stick to push my way in as much as I can. The door only opens a little. What could be blocking the way always escapes me. He never seems to change his clothes, so I don't think there are many of those lying around. Although he could not be called a poor man, a peasant is likely to have more possessions than he does, prized or otherwise. Yet, something obstructs the doorway.

"Is it sinking?" Andahar says without shifting his gaze from the mission at hand. The storm outside does not make his task any easier.

The gatekeeper of heaven must be more welcoming to the greatest sinner than Andahar is to anyone who would dare to enter his cabin. Sinner or not, today I push the door harder and begin to move a little further into the room. Even with only half of me inside, it's difficult to ignore the assault on my senses. Having lived on a ship for so long, I may have been a constant courtier to a larger variety of sharp odours than anyone else. Whether it is the stench of moisture and mould where he lives, the barely edible, gnarly-smelling meat on his plate, or the clothes soaked in bodily fluids on his men, a sailor would be damned if he stopped to think. Or smell.

But Andahar's cabin is unbearable. The air is stale. It reeks of sweat and an overpowering wetness. His foul breath fills the small chamber, stinking of meat and rum. Lots of rum. I can't help but let out a cough as I squeeze through from behind him and open the window, testing the limits of my courage.

He glares at me before getting up and slamming it shut. He sits down again, takes a huge gulp from the black bottle, re-adjusts his position, and resumes attending to his immediate objective. Although I have been trying my best to avoid it, my eyes meet his neck. I shut them immediately. How I hate seeing that crinkled leathery skin, which creeps out from under his dirty tunic as if it means to antagonise me and set ablaze the little peace I have left.

I take a deep breath and try again. "We dock at Corcusia, the city of dreams."

"Ah." A glimpse of joy runs across his face, making sure to vanish as quickly as it arrived. He lights the pipe and turns towards me.

"Tell me, oh captain, do these eyes look like they need more dreams?"

I don't know what bothers me more, his back or those eyes. They reflect a dark emptiness. A blackness so deep, I know not where it ends. An abyss of misery. They used to be brown, a beautiful dark brown. Now, you can very clearly see in them—nothing. I am often plagued by the thought that if I inspected a dead man's eyes, they would look exactly like his. But I stop myself. I would rather try to forget than find yet another bleak truth about my brother's present state.

Yes. Beneath that unkept beard, the matted hair, and the perpetual intoxication lie the remains of the man who was once my brother. It's hard to believe that he is the same man who cared for me after my accident.

"Let's go out tomorrow. A change of scenery might be good," I say, hoping that the gods will smile upon me today.

"You may leave now," he mutters, blowing a ring of smoke towards the ceiling.

"Is seven years not long enough?" I foolishly allow some of my helplessness to slip through.

Now, *my* hands are trembling, my mouth a little dry, as I continue to scorn the Goddess of Luck.

"How dare you?" He gets up in a fit of rage and hurls the chair against the wall. "Get out of my sight!" he shouts, pointing at the door.

I look down, lean on my stick and squeeze out of his chambers. Soon enough, the door is slammed. I hear the barrel being dragged back into its place. I should remember that the next time we go to the trouble of arranging for his rum.

His hostility no longer bothers me, nor does his anger. These are merely ways to make me stop coming. To make me give up. What *does* bother me are the countless days of silence that screech through the recesses of my soul. Although I would like for him to speak to me, I shudder at the thought of knowing what goes on inside that mind of his.

The winds are a little calmer as I limp onto the deck to ensure we are on course. Corcusia. I have been there many a time, but I cannot leave it to anyone else. Not this once. After a short inspection, I make my way to my chambers. My leg hurts, but tonight my mind is not with me. It's out there, swimming in the ocean of possibilities.

Could it finally happen?

There is a knock on my door.

"Who is it?"

"It is me Master, Ulgar. I bring your medicine."

"Oh yes, my boy, bring it in."

I sit on my bed with my leg stretched out. If the herbs are not applied by this time, I might as well banish myself to the dungeons of despair for the rest of the night.

The storm outside is remarkably beautiful. The ship always goes silent on nights like these. No sounds of drunken singing and dancing. And none of the screaming that comes along with the games of dice echoes from the quarters. Only a storm, or the loss of a man to the disease, engenders the eeriness that engulfs the ship.

For me, the roaring sky and the sound of rain lashing against the mast are triggers of little wonder. The fresh rain saves me from drinking the horrible water stored in those ale-laced barrels. I remember how Master Yaromi chided me. "Never trust a merchant who doesn't like his ale." However, I would rather not be trusted than be any more out of my senses than I already am. Moreover, after looking at Andahar, the thought of alcohol boils my blood. Even if there are only traces of it in the water.

Tonight, the weather seems angrier than usual, as if nature is telling me to shed the little bit of hope secretly building in my heart. We rise on the back of one angry wave and get flicked off the top like an unwanted insect, straight down into the belly of another. Up again and then down, continuously riding a furious sea of mountains. Lightning illuminates the grey clouds that envelop us, obscuring even a glimpse of the dark face of death, which could be lurking just ahead. I have not a worry though, not this time. This time, Corcusia has to be different.

"Is there a problem, Master?" Ulgar asks, trying to maintain his balance.

"A problem? Where?" I am pulled back into my chambers and immediately turn towards my safe.

Ulgar maintains a confused expression.

"Go on, boy, what's the problem?" My heart is beating a little faster. Could I have missed something? No, it cannot be. We sail as per plan. The load is full. The ship is heavy enough to ride out the storm. The men are all inside and protected. Most importantly, my safe is intact. What in the heavens could stop us now?

"No—no problem, Master," he adds nervously.

I don't understand him and shift my gaze to the porthole, back into the raging storm. The city lamps are not yet visible. It must be the clouds. But I can sense it. We are not too far now. That this storm is so bad tells me something good is coming soon.

"May I apply the herbs now, Master?"

"We reach Corcusia tomorrow," I whisper, staring into the distance.

"Will we conduct large business there, once again?"

"Business?"

"Selling the artefacts you sourced, Master?"

"Oh, right." I had almost forgotten about those.

"May I apply the herbs, Master?" the boy says, looking at me strangely.

"What? No—no herbs for me today."

"But Master, how will you—"

"Please shut the door on your way out."

I am awake long after my candle has gone out, partly due to the pain but more because of the hollow pit in my stomach. It is not from the rocking of the ship, but from the anxiety that grips my being. My mind is playing tricks, throwing questions at me as incessantly as the rain that falls from the sky, as if determined to douse the little flame of hope that is trying hard to stay alive. And that is the most painful thing about hope. It comes with the fear of losing it.

What if it is all false? What if it doesn't work? What if there really is no other way?

I lay on my bed, doing my best to fend off the attack. For the first time in all my days, I wish the pain in my leg was worse, for it would at least shift my attention from the unbearable mutiny inside.

*

"Thank you for seeing me, Andahar. In the last four days, the runners have managed to sell and deliver most of our goods, making it a lucrative docking."

"What do you want from me?" he says, aimlessly looking through the porthole behind me.

I know that look. In ten seconds, he will stop listening to me and in less than a minute, he will walk away.

"Andahar, although this has been a successful visit, one valuable artefact still needs to be delivered."

I get up, my knee throbs as if it has been shot with an arrow, but I manage to reach the safe. I struggle on my way back. As I pause for a moment, I close my eyes and take a deep breath to ease the pain. When I open them, I am greeted by a rare look of gentleness in Andahar's horrible eyes. He lends me a helping hand to get back in my chair.

I hold up the velvet bag. "I need you to deliver this extremely valuable box to the King of Templetron, who lives atop the Mountains of Templetron. It is a ride of about sixty days," I blurt out as quickly as I can.

My brother's face eases back into his habitual frown. "Find another errand boy."

The sweat dripping from my forehead betrays my attempt to appear calm.

"Andahar, the goods are much too valuable to be entrusted to an errand boy! Besides, this is an arduous journey. It will take the strength and integrity of a warrior, quite like yourself."

I notice his jaw tightening.

"I am no warrior," he grits his teeth while looking straight into my eyes.

"You are the only man here who can accomplish this expedition. And maybe, a journey off this ship is… is what you need."

I am doing it again. Poking the dragon.

"Do not tell me what I need!" he darts back at me.

"I promised the king that the box would be delivered to him within sixty days."

"Never again will I do anything for a king," he says, preparing to leave my cabin.

"Andahar—Andahar, please."

He stops and sighs deeply, exhaling more than a whiff of toxic rum.

"I have spent ten years searching for this priceless object. It was the final wish of Master Yaromi. You know better than anyone, that I was a nobody. Worse. A cripple. We belong to a warrior tribe, for goodness' sake! Do you know what it means to be a cripple when your role is to fight battles, win wars, and earn glory? Were it not for Master Yaromi, I would have lived my life as an outcast—a man who lived off the work of others— a burden. A man banished to the lowest level of society, forever labelled as one who could not fulfil his duty. Would anyone care that the accident was not my choice? I will not deny that you stood by me and cared for me, but Master Yaromi taught me that a different life was possible. I shudder to think of the existence I would have had If he had not found me. If he had not taught me the ways of a merchant."

If I didn't know him any better, his expression would have told me he wasn't listening. "He never asked me for anything, but the way he spoke of this box— the importance of it reaching the King of Templetron— this is the only way I can repay him for the grace he showered on me. And I gave him my word."

Before he can so much as blink, I pull the box out from its cover and place it on the table, hoping it will do the rest.

It is enchanting. A small golden box studded with tiny stones—rubies, diamonds, blue and yellow sapphires, red coral, cat's eye, pearls and hessonite encircling an ancient emblem: two upright lions holding a five-symbolled crest. A trident and a mace cross diagonally at the centre to form four sections. At the top, is a flame, at the bottom, a conch shell, and on either side, sits a lotus flower. The whole emblem emits an inexplicable golden hue.

Andahar's eyebrows rise the slightest bit as he stares at the box. Even he finds it difficult to ignore its mystical pull.

I put my hand on his, and he gently pulls away before I say, "Do it for my honour, Andahar. I may not have become a warrior, but the values of our tribe run deep within me. Help me to repay my debt to Master Yaromi, lest I die a man without virtue."

Is that what a crack looks like? "You can leave tomorrow, at the break of da—"

He picks up the bag and the box, and leaves my chambers without a word.

Andahar

I am tired. It has been seven years since I got off that ship. But how does it matter? On it or off, the only thing I have left is my brother. I think I was a little too harsh on him a few days ago. Actually, I am hard on him most of the time. But no, I don't understand what he wants, and I don't care what he expects of me. He should know better by now. The foolish man looks to me to protect his honour. Me?

My eyes take a while getting used to the light as I walk down the pier. I wonder if they will ever adjust at all. I can already feel the sweat rolling down my back. The sun is so harsh, showcasing its strength to creatures who can do nothing in return. A weak being. Doesn't it know the Code of Valour? "Never attack an unarmed mortal." Hypocrisy, that code was.

The sky must give the water its colour. Sapphire. Waves quickly crawl onto the sand and leave just as sheepishly, as if aware of their folly, conveniently leaving on another the weeds they brought with them. Another hollow one from the Code of Valour: "Uphold the ideal justice." Obviously, there is no justice, not even in nature. Fools we are to expect dreary humans to uphold it. What does it even mean? "Ideal justice?" Ideal for whom? Rubbish.

As I continue my walk from the pier to the city gates, the number of people I encounter increases sharply. Too many for my comfort. Some men unload objects from the ships while several others follow merchants, carrying troves and boxes. Some lead what appear to be finely bred horses. In the blistering sun, one merchant wears a coat. I wonder who would want to trade with this madman?

There is one particularly offensive man, his hair dripping with oil, loud-mouthed and foul-tongued. His lips are red, probably from chewing betel leaf. He is shorter than every single one of the slaves he leads. Men and women alike. With one order in his unusually shrill voice, his men give the slaves a lashing. Chained together at their hands and feet, they probably know not what they did to deserve it. The clanking sound that echoes as the chains hit the ground reminds me of yet another meaningless code: "Protect the innocent."

The city is walled. It lies within a huge stone fortress nestled between two overarching cliffs. On each of them, I see what appear to be watch towers. Puny guards stand with their arrows aimed at the gates, fooling themselves with their pretentious strength. Have any of them ever shot an arrow? And what is so worthy of protection, anyway?

Maybe they will look at me as a murderer and finally experience the joy of an arrow flying from their bows, relieving me, once and for all. If only it weren't for

Ned-Har. I cannot leave him alone in this world, not after everything. Unless the ship were to sail into a storm and sink, taking him along with it. Or, if he were to die of the disease. It would make it all much simpler. Then I would gladly give these toy guards the pleasure of killing a man.

There are two queues to enter the city. One for men with goods, and one for those without. The one with goods is far longer. It appears that men from various parts of the world come to this city to make their fortunes. The officials at the gates collect a toll. The short man with the slaves walks to the front of the goods queue, much to the dismay of the others. He points at the slaves while exchanging a few words with the two gatekeeping officials. Then he signals his men, who bring out a young woman in chains, crying and begging, and deliver her to the officials' little chambers. While they wait outside guarding the door, the slave monger and the rest of the group are allowed to pass through without payment of a toll. One of the gatekeeping officials and the slave monger share a hearty laugh as the other throws stones at the slaves, mocking their helplessness. My blood boils. I would crush their heads right now if I had not a task to complete. The code should have been: "Protect the oppressor and punish the oppressed." Then it would have made complete sense.

I am pulled out of my thoughts by two guards half my size who direct me out of the queue towards an official sitting in the corner watching everyone. He reminds me of an Alaunt hunting dog, trained to see only what his master wants him to see, but with far more suspicion.

"Origin?" he barks at me.

"The sea." I watch the slaves climb the stairs that go up to the city. The clanging rings in my ears.

The first man I have spoken to in many years. Apart from Ned-Har, of course.

"The sea? Where do you belong?" He bangs his fist on the table.

"Nowhere," I reply firmly.

"What could a man like you want in the Golden City?" He raises his gruff voice.

I turn towards him and look straight at his face.

He shifts in his chair. I sense the guards behind me taking a step forward.

"There is a toll to enter our city. Come back if you ever—"

I throw a couple of gold coins on his table and walk through the gates.

No one follows me.

It's a nauseating climb up the stairs to the city. The ground doesn't sway. After so many years, it's still. After climbing for a while, I reach what seems to be a ghastly, crowded street, some kind of marketplace.

Throngs of people clamour about the shops, knocking into each other. But none knock into me. On either side of the cobblestone street, all sorts of shops slope up into the distance. Even before my eyes can perceive the offerings, I am greeted by a strange scent. No, it's not the sea, not the dried fish. It's quite disagreeable. I know not if it comes from the tea in those earthen pots or the stall selling spices. I recognise cumin, pepper, and cinnamon, but there is a crowd around an orange spice, all of them screaming the word "saff-ron," as though it holds the answer to their meaningless existence. A little ahead, a food seller is cooking something in a giant pot. I see it is a broth made with some of the more potent spices his neighbour sells. I let out a cough. A perfume seller is haggling with a lady customer, taking stock of incoming goods and screaming to his assistant to spray more perfume at the entrance, all at the same time. He reminds him to use the cheap one. Revolting. The mad merchant, whom I saw earlier, passes by and pushes his way through to a shop a little further up the street. Someone who appears to be the owner speaks animatedly, gesturing him to hurry. The merchant's men begin to empty three troves of dry fruits into giant vessels placed outside. I can understand the shopkeeper's fury, for I have heard Ned-Har repeat that morning trade is the best and if you would like to deny yourself money, be late. And I realise that I've chosen the worst time to enter this dreadful place. But what could I do? I had to leave immediately.

The street is chaotic and congested. The people all look the same to me. They seem to be engaged in a screaming contest. Their volume decreases only if their eyes meet me. I pass a shop selling colourful scarves ranging from a horrible dark orange to the ugliest light pink, an irritatingly bright yellow to a distracting deep red. I wonder whom to pity more, the sellers or the people who buy them. Whether it is the jewellery shop, the moneylender's premises, the lamp seller's stall or any other place in this horrid market, it is filled with the continuous sound of chatter and giggles, squabbling and haggling. And if that is not enough, there are the sellers who narrate absurd stories about the origins of their worthless goods. The only thing familiar is the faint calling of the usually loud seagulls.

The street is lined with short stone buildings, all with red roofs rising along its slope, probably the homes of the shopkeepers. The main street continues to meander up, giving onto narrow alleyways at regular intervals. After walking around aimlessly for a short while, I decide to move away from the crowds, for that is where I will find the place I most need at the moment. I enter one of the dirtiest lanes I can find, almost needing to squeeze through. Rats scurry across. I don't mind them. There were enough of them on the ship. I recognise the stench here—poor drainage. A man is lying on the ground, seemingly unconscious, his clothes tattered and dirty, which tells me I am walking in the right direction. As I cross over him, he looks up at me and smiles, revealing partially broken teeth, then breaks into an uncontrolled hum and indicates to me to take a right up ahead. One recognises the other, perhaps. There should be a code on this, for it would be followed in every instance. "Always help a fellow drunkard find his ale." I follow his instructions and come onto a lonely lane with a strange odour. Oddly, the few buildings in this lane have no doors. Instead, curtains cover the entrances.

"It's still afternoon, honey!" I look up to find that the croaky voice belongs to a harsh-looking middle-aged woman with a big build. Her face is powdered white, her lips a shabby red and her eyes kohl smudged. She strokes her frizzy hair while looking at me from one of the windows. "Won't you let them get some rest?"

I ignore her.

"I can wake them if you'd like," she adds, casually looking at her nails.

A short distance ahead, I come to a dead end where I see two men with covered heads quickly entering a building.

"Don't lose all your money in there, darling. You won't get any of my girls for free," the lady at the window screams from behind.

Just the place I needed, the tavern.

As I make my way inside, I find myself in a small passage with steps leading down to a doorway. The air is musty. Standing at the threshold, I see a space much larger than I expected from the size of the door. A doorkeeper tries to block my way, but I push him aside while trying to be gentle. He calls out to me to stop, and just as I am about to turn around, the barkeeper signals him to let me in. The tavern is largely empty, apart from the two men who entered before me. Long wooden tables lined with vacant chairs lie close to each other. A likely hazard as the sun sets. Dimly lit lamps hang from the ceiling, which is as low as one would expect. The big jugs on the tables are empty for now.

I go over to the bar where the barkeeper, likely the tavern's owner, is wiping a tumbler. He is a burly old man with a curly beard that nearly covers his face, giving him the look of a bear that has lived too long amongst deranged humans. Without saying a word, he draws ale from a barrel behind him and places the tumbler in front of me. Finally, a man who does not have the need to talk. I sit there for a few hours, gulping down one ale after another.

Unless it is my imagination, the tavern keeper passes something to me from time to time. First, a broth, which is later removed untouched and replaced with a piece of roasted chicken, which has since been exchanged for a small piece of cheese and a shrivelled bitter orange. I wonder what will appear If I do not partake of this, either. Whenever I look up, I find his attention stuck on me with an unwanted look of concern. I am beginning to dislike this man.

With my head resting on my palm, I fix my gaze on the tumbler of ale. The sun must be close to setting for more footsteps echo off the floor, more chairs are dragged noisily, more clumsy conversations without a care for the broken silence. As the evening progresses, the room is filled with the sound of jugs colliding, ale spilling on the floor and screaming over discordant singing, which only gets louder and louder.

"ATTENTION! ATTENTION!"

The cheese and bitter orange are no longer on the bar, likely eaten by the two men who now sit on either side of me.

"I SAID, ATTENTIONNNNNNNNNNN!" A shrill voice penetrates the din in the tavern, abruptly bringing it to a halt. I recognise the voice, though not fondly, and turn to see a short, red-mouthed and oily-haired, drunken man standing on a table, barely able to maintain his balance. It is him—the slave monger.

"This... this man over here...." he points at a man drinking from a seemingly empty tumbler. "This man says he doesn't know what is... is special about this city of Corcusia," he slurs on, making me feel as though a pestilent worm with a thousand feet is crawling over my body.

"I promised him... you noble crowd, and I will enlighten him. So, tell me, my friends, what do you like about Corcusia?" he yells to the crowd amongst cheers.

One man stands up, lifts his drink almost to the ceiling, and screams, "The womennnnnn!" The crowd breaks into a large cheer, banging on the tables, making all sorts of sounds. The slave monger laughs and stomps his feet on the table like a madman.

The tavern keeper is not too happy, but he does nothing and continues to keep a keen watch.

The man sitting next to me speaks up. "May I add my opinion, kind gentlemen?"

"Go on, philosopher, let us hear it," the slave monger says on behalf of the crowd.

The philosopher adjusts his pointed hat before beginning. "My dear, kind men." Scattered laughter.

"Oh, spare us the misery," shouts another of the drunk men.

"Your fair city of Corcusia is a place of great culture." Scattered applause.

Irritation is building on the slave monger's face. "Very well, who else would like to speak—"

"But it is said that if the people's hearts are pure, barren land will be blissful. And if their hearts are full of hatred and greed, no land can be sacred." The philosopher continues adding his unwelcome opinion amidst voices demanding that he be quiet or leave.

The philosopher puts his drink down and stands up to argue with some befuddled men, leaving unattended a book and a little pouch.

"Oh, you philosophers take it all too seriously," the slave monger snaps. "What I like here is how thieves are punished. The filth rob from us... merchants who serve society. And the Corcusian law puts them to the thumb screw. They should be thrown onto the chair of needles, I reckon. Boiled in hot water for even thinking about stealing my... our money again. Across all the lands I have travelled, the torture of dirty men is the best in this city."

The men stand up, raise their jugs and scream animatedly. They lift the slave monger onto their shoulders and dance around.

I take the opportunity to quietly pick up the philosopher's pouch and place it beneath the slave monger's chair, amidst the commotion.

"And what would you say if someone entered the city without paying the toll?" I scream.

The tavern goes silent. All eyes are on me. The tavern keeper breaks into a little frown as he looks towards two vicious-looking men, probably watchmen from the City Guard.

"Uh, he... he must most certainly be punished," the slave monger stutters, "he must be thrown into prison... and... and... put onto the rack. Or dunked into the waters," he continues rambling.

"And, what about being a slave monger? No robbing there, eh?" I ask.

He must be well known, for many in the crowd let out a gasp. The slave monger frowns.

"Would that be slave monger or mongrel? Ah. Too much ale." I snigger as I take my seat.

The murmur in the crowd increases.

"It is called the human trade," he clears his throat, suddenly not as drunk. "A service to society, removing the most unworthy vermin from amidst us of pure blood and putting them into jobs best suited to pests like them. They don't deserve to be—"

"MY POUCH!" the philosopher screams. "There is a thief here! A thief!"

The watchmen stand up. One blocks the door while the other begins moving through the crowd.

"It had all my money, I... I... sold my belongings to travel to Corcusia!" He begins to sob loudly.

"Poor fellow," the crowd sighs, quite sympathetic for a drunken bunch.

"The menace of society, thieves! He must be caught and—" the slave monger cuts short his painful rant as a watchman bends down beside his chair. "What do you think you are—"

"Is this your pouch?" The watchman holds it up to the philosopher.

"YES! Yes, kind gentleman!" the philosopher yelps and rushes towards the watchman.

All eyes turn towards the slave monger. The watchman towers over him.

"Why… why do you look at me?" He frowns nervously at the watchman.

"He must be punished!" a man screams.

"Do you know who I am? How dare you—"

"Hypocrite!" someone adds while dealing him a blow. A commotion builds up as the watchman picks him up by his collar and takes him outside.

The crowd cheers, and soon after, the singing resumes, and the room returns to its original bustle.

"He will be gone a while." The tavern keeper looks at me and smiles, without saying more.

I do not react and get up to leave. The slave mongrel deserved worse.

"You can stay here tonight, room's upstairs," he points towards a staircase in the corner.

I nod, and after a little more than my usual share of the drink, I somehow manage to make my way up the steps, not without any damage, though. I knock into the hideous one-eyed man who stares out from a painting on the wall, as if judging the lives of those who climb these stairs. How am I to blame? The dingy staircase was certainly not built for normal human beings.

On the upper floor, I find a single room, unsurprisingly small, lit by the flame of a short candle that appears to be drowning in a pool of its tears, not permitted to die. A feeling I am quite familiar with. The little window is tightly shut, just as I prefer. As I fall onto the bed, I am greeted by a whiff of mould and sweat. A gift from the unknown man who lay here before me, and soon I fall asleep, despite the jarring noises from below.

*

The houses are burning, the dogs are barking wildly. The cold night is hot and rife with the smell of smoke from the debris left behind. My heart is pounding loudly, but I am overpowered by the shrieking silence of disbelief. I see nothing but fire rising in the distance. They made sure I could see it through the window of my cell. The dizziness makes me fall to the ground. I take out her handkerchief. It smells of her. It was only last night she slept in my arms. If I could stretch time just a little, she would still be with me. This cannot be true, how can she... How can Narcia be gone? I scream into the handkerchief. The reality of her absence has become so loud, it makes me sick. My stomach churns. I vomit, nearly choking on my distress. It feels like

I am stuck in a horrible nightmare, one from which I am unable to awaken. I put her handkerchief to my face again. Inhaling her scent might make me forget what I saw, if only for a moment.

I wake up with a jolt to terrifying emptiness. Breathless. Again. My face is covered with her handkerchief. But it no longer carries her fragrance. I stagger towards the window and desperately try to open it with my trembling hands. I put my head out into the night sky. It is much quieter now. Quiet enough to hear the grunting of a man from the brothel next door. A gentle breeze blows onto my face but fails to console me. Despite my exhaustion, sleep won't come back now.

Elar

"Hurry up, boy!"

It wasn't my fault. I was up on time. I woke Master, too. But no, it *is* my fault. Who would say it isn't? I try to keep up, but the trove is heavier today, and the stones are slippery.

NOISE, SPLATTER, FALL.

The trove hits the ground so loudly I can hear it over the ringing in my ears. I feel a blow. A kick. Straight to my stomach. Before I can catch my breath, I am dangling in the air, my skin rubbing against the rough wall behind me. I try hard to open my eyes.

"You useless, miserable excuse for a servant! Pack it all up! If we miss our ship, you will go hungry for a week."

He drops me to the ground. I can't think. If only I could race as fast as my heart right now.

"The poor boy is hurt."

A deep voice behind me. I don't turn to tell him that it does not matter. I must gather the things. It is my fault. Master will punish me.

"Poor boy? Cursed I am to have him for a servant," Master says, with a wave of his hand.

"Cursed he is to have a master like you," says the man.

Am I dreaming? Who would dare talk to my master that way? Doesn't he know he will be punished?

I turn to see a big man. A stained tunic hangs from his broad shoulders down to his knees. His sandals are laced up to his calves. The hood of his tunic loosely covers his head. Long, matted hair falls to his chest. His beard hides what might be a very handsome face. He looks strong, like a fighter. There is something scary about his eyes. The frown on his face makes it worse. He surely must carry a weapon in the sack he slings over his shoulder.

Master is frozen. I know that look. He is angry. Very angry.

"The boy is my servant! What I do with him is my business, and you would do well to stay out of it," Master shouts.

"You would do well to treat him better." The man is towering over Master. Do I see sweat on his forehead? No, it cannot be. I do my best to gather the carpets. It pains me, but sleeping hungry will hurt more.

Master hurries ahead, and I sit beside the trove gazing at the man who spoke for me. No one has done that before. Why did he? Has he mistaken me for someone else?

"Hurry up, Elar!"

Master hollers at me in that sharp voice that makes my hair stand. Do I know this man? Did he know my father? He helps me stand and asks if I am all right.

"What in the devil's name are you doing, boy? Get here!"

For the first time, I do not obey my master.

"Get moving NOW or find yourself a new master! Be warned, no one will hire an insolent, disobedient and lazy boy like you."

"I will," the big man says.

My head must surely be injured. Is this really happening?

"Boy, you will pay for this when the mountain man has no money to feed you. Go, die on the streets. What do I care?" Master spits on the ground, muttering under his breath while rushing ahead.

"Master, please…" I make a feeble attempt, but he does not look back and continues to push the trove in a desperate attempt to reach the ship.

"You will be better off without a master like that." The big man speaks to me in a gentle tone that makes me uncomfortable. Is he being pleasant because of what he plans to do to me? Could he be worse than the merchant?

"I will send you to serve my brother, a merchant whose ship is docked here at the port."

No, no! Not someone else. And not another merchant. What if he keeps me hungry? But how much worse can he be? Those ships are infested with rats. Well, there are plenty of them on land, as well. No, I want to serve this big man. He is kind. Say something, Elar. Open your mouth before it is too late! "Master... can I... not be in your service?" I smile nervously.

"No," he says, sternly. "Go to the port and find the ship of Ned-Har. When you meet him, tell him that Andahar sent you." He pauses. "Do you have some parchment?"

I rummage through my sack, find a piece of crumpled parchment and hand it to him.

"A quill?"

I have it somewhere. I search for it frantically.

"Alright, boy, let it be. Just tell him these words: The box is safe. He will know that I sent you."

I don't want to go, but I cannot question him. I must obey. I bow and hurry towards the port, turning for one last glimpse. He must be going to the fair. Remember Elar, the ship of Ned-Har. Sent by Master Andahar. The box is... safe! The box is safe.

Ned-Har

I sit at my desk. Swaying with the waves and the thoughts that won't leave me.

How will he fare on his journey? What will be the outcome? Will it be a disappointment once more? No, it cannot be. This time must be different.

Seven years ago, when I brought Andahar to the ship, I hoped time and travel would slowly settle his mind. I even foolishly believed that one day his tormented heart would mend. But season after season, he remained silent, rum, his only ally. He had been a respected warrior, used to the spoils of victory and the pleasures of life. Surely, he would tire of the ship, I thought. But he never spoke. Not even to complain of the stale meat, or the dry biscuits or the smells, or any of the innumerable perils of living at sea. I had hoped that, perhaps, the constant swaying would make him sick. But no, he continued to drown himself in rum when he had it, and cheap ale when he didn't. He remained in his cabin day and night, not even disembarking at the many ports where we docked, those forays on land that relieved the harsh life of a sailor. From attempting to speak with him, to sending him exotic women, I did everything. Everything I could to free him from the prison he had banished himself to. Neither did the women gain entry into his cabin, nor I into the cockles of his heart. Even if I hadn't heard his screams at night, his eyes would have told me the real story. What could I do? The pain of my shattered knee was nothing compared to the pain of watching my brother slowly kill himself, day after day.

On my travels, I consulted shamans, oracles and famed healers. As advised, I added potions to his rum, placed enchanted ornaments under his bed— even chanted incantations. But none of these brought lasting relief. Still, I persisted, even tried to ignore the gnawing voice that told me nothing I did would heal a man who did not wish to be healed. And I prayed and prayed that one day divinity would show him the light.

Maybe this time...

"Master, is it finally time for Master Andahar?" Ulgar interrupts my thoughts, as if peering into my mind.

"What do you mean?" I shift slightly in my chair.

"He left the ship after seven years, Master. It is all anyone can talk about."

I smile. This must be a sign.

"What is different this time, Master?" He looks at me expectantly.

I pause for a moment before answering him. "Do you remember our last visit to India?"

"The business with the Maharaja?"

"Oh Ulgar, what is your obsession with 'business'! You have been serving merchants far too long."

He looks down at his feet.

"Look beyond, Ulgar. Much more than business took place in India. The evening after I delivered the jewels, I was a guest at the Maharaja's palace. A lavish meal was followed by an evening of enchanting music and dance, which nearly made me forget my constant distress. Late into the night, I was escorted back to my chambers, and just as I finished applying the herbs, I heard a knock at the door. I was startled and asked who it was. No one replied. The knocking continued. Then I heard a whisper. 'Ned-Har sahib.' I put my ear to the door. 'Ned-Har sahib.'

"I recognised the voice and opened the door ever so slightly to find it was Mishra-ji, holding a lamp."

"Who was Mishra-ji, Master?"

"He managed the Royal House of Artefacts. With a serious expression, he said, 'I apologise for the intrusion, Ned-Har sahib, but it is a matter of grave importance.' I asked if I was in some trouble. He replied, 'With all due respect, Ned-Har sahib, have you not been in trouble for some time now?' I was taken aback. 'I may have the solution to your problem,' he said. 'I can be of help to you, if you come with me and prove your heart.' I was confused. 'I don't understand, Mishra-ji.' 'You are a man of faith. If you find the courage to come with me, you may find the answers to the questions you have been asking.'

"I was beginning to feel frightened, but I assured him that I had no troubles, although, at that point, I may have been convincing myself more than him. He replied, 'In that case, forgive my intrusion.' He folded his hands and turned to leave.

"Something made me stop him. 'Mishra-ji,' I said, 'please wait. Where must we go?'

"'Sahib,' he replied, 'it is not my place to speak of this. If sire were able to trust in life, he might find what he has been seeking.'

"'And I will have to... prove my heart?' Mishra-ji smiled and nodded."

Ulgar interrupts me, "But Master were you not..."

I glare at him and continue my tale. "I do not know what made me trust him, and the very next day, we were on our way. It rained during the entire two-day journey through the dense jungle. Long vines cascaded from tall, thick, ancient trees, and the dense undergrowth made it difficult for us to walk. In places, it was marshy and slippery. Not to mention the blood-sucking leeches that stuck to my flesh. We carried no food or water, and from time to time, Mishra-ji plucked small berries that kept me surprisingly satiated. Even a few drops of rainwater collected on the leaves were enough to quench my thirst.

"I was unsettled, not knowing what sort of test I would face. When I asked Mishra-ji, his response was always the same: 'Your patience will be rewarded.'"

Ulgar asks, "But Master, were you not nervous?"

"The unexpected trumpeting of elephants resounding through the jungle, or the mighty bison darting from the bushes was enough to make anyone's hair stand. But Mishra-ji remained unperturbed. He bowed to any animal that came close, as if he knew them personally. I was very wary. At one point, a peahen suddenly flew across my face, squealing. I screamed and gripped Mishra-ji, who only laughed and shook his head. He told me not to worry, for the jungle knew where we were going, and no harm could befall us.

"At one time, I even thought I might be sacrificed in a tribal ritual!" I laugh, but Ulgar doesn't flinch. "When we stopped for the night, I realised that for the first time in years, my knee did not pain me at all. And I could not help but think... the raindrops, the berries, my knee. Were these divine signs?

"After two days of travelling through the jungle, we reached an extremely dense area. We had to walk through thick bamboo whose leaves scratched our faces. The creaking of the stalks was so loud, it almost felt as if we were inside one giant bamboo plant. Soon, we reached a place from where we could go no further. Mishra-ji recited something in a tongue foreign to me, and after a few moments... pin drop silence.

"Then a deep voice thundered, as though it came from the heavens. 'Welcome, Ned-Har of the Blue Mountains. Thus far, you have shown extraordinary courage and faith, but before you continue your journey, you must answer three questions:

"'Which is greater, love for oneself or love for another?'

"I paused to think, then answered, 'The deepest form of love cannot distinguish between oneself and another.'

"The deep voice asked the second question: 'Who is the most knowledgeable of all?'

"'He who knows Nothing,' I replied.

"Then the final question: 'Who is the wealthiest of all?'

"This one was tough, but after briefly considering, I replied, 'He who has enough.'"

"And then, Master?" Ulgar's eyes reflect an innocent wonder.

"Pin drop silence once again. It was as if everything had momentarily ceased to exist. Then I heard a voice behind me. 'Well, hello, Ned-Har.' I turned to find a young-looking sage sitting cross-legged under a giant tree with a brown cat in his lap. He was bald, and his face was glowing. His eyes were soft and seemed all-knowing, as though he had seen everything that could be seen, as though he was beyond the illusions of this world. He wore two powder dots on his forehead, a red one between his brows, and a yellow a little above. I remember admiring how handsome he looked in his saffron robe.

"Mishra-ji bowed before him, and I did the same. The youthful appearance of the sage contradicted his presence, which felt many centuries old. He spoke gently. 'Born in a warrior community and having been not only an orphan but also an outcast, you went beyond your pain to find your inner voice. Under the care of a kind master, you worked harder than those blessed with an able body and earned immense respect and wealth. But that is not your biggest strength. Instead, your greatest fortune is your ability to connect with your heart, which is the first thing one loses when difficulties arise.' He looked at me with eyes full of love while petting the cat, who appeared to enjoy his divine company.

"The sage continued to recall intimate details of my life, from my thoughts as a child to the secrets of the trade Master Yaromi taught me. How could he have known? I was astonished, while at the same time, unsurprised.

"'No journey is meaningless,' he said, 'for if you had not experienced each phase of your life, you would not be able to connect all the little dots and find the beauty that was waiting to be discovered. And like the rest of us, your brother is on his own journey.' He paused, closed his eyes, and whispered something while holding his palm towards the sky. As he opened his eyes, a stunning jewelled box appeared in his hand.

"He beckoned me to come closer, and as I did, I was mesmerised by the heavenly scent that emanated from him. He handed me the box and said prophetically, 'Go to the city of Corcusia and send your brother on the next phase of his journey. He must take this box to the Mountains of Templetron.' With tears streaming down my cheeks, I bowed before him in gratitude, and he nodded with an ever gentle, humble smile.

"Then his smile became playful, and he leaned forward saying, 'Don't mind the three questions you were asked. You do not need to pass a test to receive help, Mishra-ji and I were just having some fun.' The sage winked at Mishra-ji, and they burst into soft laughter."

Ulgar asks, "What was in the box, Master?"

There is a knock at my door, and he goes to investigate.

"A boy has come to see you," he reports. "He says he was sent by Master Andahar."

By Andahar? "Bring him in."

A scrawny boy appears. He is neither short nor tall. His ears are so pointy, they might have done better on a kitten. A dirty cloth bag hangs loosely across his chest, partially covering a grey tunic which appears older than he does and a few sizes bigger than he needs. His head is bruised, teeth stained with blood, but his eyes have an innocent spark, hard to find in a boy his age. Looking down at his feet, he fidgets with his nails.

"I am Elar of Corcusia, servant to… sent by the kind Master Andahar to serve Master Ned-Har," he stammers.

"Serve Master Ned-Har?" Ulgar is indignant. "Master, this boy is a fraud. He carries no note, no evidence that Master Andahar sent him. We must—"

"The box is safe! The box is safe!" the panicked boy squeals.

Ulgar and I exchange a glance, my eyes not as wide as his. I gesture to him to give us a moment and ask the boy to explain. He blurts out everything about the life he has led.

He is the only child of parents who served a wealthy carpet merchant and his family for many years. They lived on the merchant's land, and while his father tended to the merchant's person, his mother looked after the kitchen. Most of the day, he worked with his mother and learnt the art of cooking. Although the merchant treated them poorly, he was reasonably happy until his mother fell ill. She seemed to suffer from influenza but soon began to vomit blood, and after a few weeks, she died, leaving the boy with his father.

I feel sorry for the boy. The agony of losing a mother must surely be greater than the pain of not having one. Just as he began to emerge from his grief, his father was killed in an accident. Alone in the world, he was forced to travel with the merchant, selling carpets and becoming the object of his constant abuse. He was always occupied with his duties, and in the rare moments he had to himself, he flipped through the pages of his only book, *The Legendary Legends of the Central World*. He proudly shows me the tattered volume and tells me that an old storyteller gave it to him. This man, who lived in a town frequented by the carpet merchant, was his only friend. The boy does not know how to read but claims to remember every single legend and the symbols attached to them, as taught by the storyteller.

Growing up alone in the world must have been traumatic. I had Andahar, at least. I drift into my thoughts as he continues with his stories, some relevant, others not. The secret ingredient in his favourite chicken soup, his distrust of merchants, the sadness he felt when he walked away from Andahar, and his strong desire to serve him. I interrupt him gently, and soon enough, he goes on to tell me what happened this morning. He continues to talk while I scribble a note on a piece of parchment.

"Go back to Andahar," I say. "Serve him well, Elar. He needs you." I hand him the note. "And don't tell him I said so."

The boy is dumbstruck and looks at me to make sure he heard correctly.

"Go now! Find him before it's too late."

He dashes off as fast as he can, then skids to a stop and turns to bow before racing away again.

Andahar

I walk through the meandering streets to reach an archway that opens onto a large, crowded square. At its centre, sits an imposing bell tower that overlooks the ongoing fair. There are stalls everywhere, filled with a variety of merchandise. Multiple performers roam the square. There are dancers and actors. Musicians accompanied by dancing bears. Clowns blow through rings of fire while acrobats show off their skills. Jugglers perform outside some stalls, attracting quite a crowd. A few artists showcase their work, while some others draw portraits, mostly of children whose parents urge them to sit still. A few men loudly narrate stories of God to the hopeless group gathered before them. Most of the people at the fair fill themselves with food, drink and useless conversation. To add to the cacophony, there are hordes of peasants who lead their horses, goats, and sheep towards the livestock market, while others push carts filled with sacks of grain. Watchmen survey the square for troublemakers.

I take a deep breath and make my way towards a craftsman's stall. His apprentice whispers something in his ear, and he gives me a quick but careful glance. "We are not serving customers today," he says. It is absurd, for I have observed him welcoming every visitor before me, showing them poorly designed bows and wasteful pots. I ask no questions and move on to the next stall, a bread maker.

"I am looking for the Mountains of Templetron." What looked like half a smile a moment earlier turns into an expression of disgust.

"The busiest day of the year, and you come along playing jokes? Off you go before I call the watchmen!" he barks like a rabid dog.

I clench my fist a little and move on to the blacksmith, who is proudly showcasing axes, armour, and horseshoes. "I can get you the most brutal knife you have ever seen," he says, welcoming me in.

"I need to know the way to the Mountains of Templetron."

"Be gone before I demonstrate my devices of torture on you, you crazy wayfarer!"

"See a physician first," says the fruit seller, heaving a deep sigh.

Next, I approach the wine seller, betting against all odds that he has some integrity. "Drunk in the day, are we?" he spits out.

I reluctantly move on to the priest who stands outside the church admiring the mosaic designs highlighted by the sunlight as it falls on the window panes. "I need directions."

"And where do you seek to go, my child?" he replies, the only politeness I have encountered so far.

"The Mountains of Templetron."

He puts his hand on my shoulder and looks at me with pity. "Don't believe everything you hear. Give your life to God and live with what you have. That is the path to joy."

I hurry out of there, cursing myself.

My quest continues with a cheese seller, an artist, a sweetmeat maker, a grain seller, a lamp seller, and a lone man with a horse. All of them have many things to say, none of which are directions.

After hearing the tower bell toll many times, I decide to make my way to a large fountain in a corner of the square, but as I walk along, the annoying feeling of being watched makes me turn around.

A lanky watchman stops a short distance away.

"I don't have time for this," I murmur to myself, continuing to walk.

"I hear you are causing mischief and harassing people," he yells.

"It is your people who are harassing me! They are as hollow as the Code of Valour. Have they never heard, 'Help those in need?'"

The watchman looks confused. "What help does a man like you need from innocent people attending a fair?" he speaks loudly, as if trying to make up in volume what he lacks in height.

"I am only asking for directions to the Mountains of Templetron," I reply.

"You want the Mountains of Templetron?"

I nod.

"Well, I want to bed the queen!"

Not more of this rubbish! I turn and continue walking.

"If I find you causing more trouble at this fair, I will—"

"YOU will—what?" I turn and take a step towards him. He jumps back, grasping the stick he carries in his belt, frantically looking around for his fellow watchmen.

"I tell you, I will be watching you," he threatens from a safe distance. "Wonder how all the fools of the world land in our great city!"

I reach the fountain where a grim-looking musician is drinking the water that cascades from the mouth of a wolf carved from marble. It would have been better had it spouted ale instead. As I sit by the fountain, the musician's face lights up. He jumps to his feet and begins to play his flute, startling the pigeons into flight. He gently kicks his empty hat towards me. I put my hand into my pouch, and his playing gets even more horrifying. His face becomes animated, as if he is consumed by the ecstasy of performing the finest tune ever heard. I start moving my hand away from the pouch, and that very face breaks into a frown, all of which is reflected in his ghastly tune, of course. I toss a gold coin up and catch it in my palm. The musician is shocked. He stops playing for a moment, takes a deep breath and his expression tells me he is about to start again, even more wildly this time.

"I am looking for a place," I speak up quickly.

"And I will play a tune that will help you find it." His eyes are glued to the coin.

"NO! You have played enough." I try hard to control my temper. The watchmen should apprehend this man. "Just tell me where I can find the Mountains of—"

"I have had enough! All day, people want to hear my melodious tunes but walk away when the time comes to reward the poor musician."

"Tell me where I can find the Mountains of Templetron, and this is yours." I raise the coin in my fingers.

"I don't know any mountains," he says.

I lower the coin and shrug my shoulders.

"Mountains… YES! The green hills. Walk down from the square and—"

"Don't take me for a fool. If I walk downhill from the square, I will reach the port."

"Not that side! The other side, stand beneath the arch, and you will see the green hills in the distance."

"The green hills? That cannot be—"

"Look, I told you what I know!"

"Is that so?" I get up to leave and his impatience turns to pleading. "That's all I know! The hills are the only thing close to mountains here. I will take you to the arch, and you will see them in the distance."

I nod and he leads the way through the animals, the peasants, performers and sellers until we reach the archway.

"Look," he says, pointing into the distance.

The street winds all the way down to merge into the meadows. There is a bridge over a river and on the other side, the meadows continue. Establishments are scattered into the distance, beyond which there are the hills. Hills? So tiny, they don't deserve to be called so.

"Please, don't play that thing." I throw him the coin and set off down the street. After a short while, I hear a familiar voice from behind.

"MASTER! MASTER!"

I turn to find Elar running towards me.

"Master... I thought I wouldn't find you," he bends over, trying to catch his breath. "I ran up all the... I have done it before, but the stairs... My head spins a little."

"Did you not find the ship?"

"I did, Master. I met Master Ned-Har. He is not like the cruel merchant who—"

"Did you not tell him what I said?" I cut short his irritating chatter.

"Yes, Master, I told him, but he sent me back." He hands me a piece of parchment.

It reads, *Brother, I appreciate your sincerity in rescuing this boy. However, I do not have a job for him. It would be most suitable for you to send him back to his former master. N*

Damn you, Ned-Har. I look at the boy.

"I was scared, Master. What if I didn't find you? The fair was full of people, all the people of all the villages and towns around Corcusia. As a child, I once got lost there, but Mother found me. I knew she would help me find you, too. Thank you, Mother!" He looks up at the sky.

I close my eyes and rub my forehead.

"I asked every trader I could find if they had seen you. One of them, umm… I think it was the wine seller. He asked me if you were big. I said yes, and then he asked if you had long hair. I was so happy. I said, 'YES, YES.' He asked if you were dirty, umm… your clothes, he asked me about your clothes. When I said yes, he said that you were a… well. I could stand there no longer. Father always taught me never to stand by and listen to foul words about your Master."

I can't believe this is happening.

"Master," he continues. "I then went to a watchman thinking they would be the best people to ask, for they know everything about everyone in Corcusia. The watchman asked the same questions as the wine seller and replied rather angrily that he had chased you through the arch and let you go only because you begged for mercy. He said he had to follow his code, so he allowed you to pass, but not without a strict warning. I thanked him and ran as fast as I could to find you. You must be careful of these watchmen, Master. They are a scary bunch of men, they can—"

"Listen, Elar, if you are to join me on my journey, remember two things: Stay out of my way and maintain silence at ALL times."

"Yes, sire, understood, sire."

"Master, would you like to take a bath?" he resumes as I continue walking. "Corcusia has hot water coming from under the ground, it can set a bad stomach right."

I keep walking.

"Would you like me to carry your sack?"

Hoping that my silence will send a message, I continue to ignore him.

"Where are we going, Master? I will go anywhere with you."

I was wrong.

"How much longer?" he asks as if we have been travelling for days.

"I don't know."

"Master... umm... Do you know where we need to go?" he asks, senselessly kicking a stone that whizzes past me.

"Aren't you supposed to be quiet?"

"Yes, yes, sire," he blurts out while kicking another stone.

We continue walking down the largely empty street.

"Master, it seems you don't know where we need to go."

Why Andahar, did you save him? The merchant was probably right.

"I could umm, help, Master. I've roamed these streets for almost fifteen years." He pauses. "But that would mean I started when I was only... a baby?" he continues mumbling.

Who is he talking to?

"Maybe a little less," he mutters. "BUT MASTER! A long, long time."

I stop and turn around. He is looking at the ground and jumps back when he bumps into me.

"If you know this place so well, tell me, oh explorer, how do we get to the Mountains of Templetron? No one other than a poor musician had the courtesy to help a wayfarer asking for directions. And that, after promising him a gold coin in return. So, we are going to the green hills. Will you please not utter another word until we get there?" Hopefully, this should make him stop.

"One gold coin? For directions? That's outrageous!" he screams.

I try to burn him down with my eyes.

"WAIT! We are going to the Mountains of Templetron?" he shrieks. "WOW! WOW!"

I heave a deep sigh and begin walking again.

"Master, did you know that the last person who went to those mountains and came back alive was the Ali of Prusse—and that was more than three hundred years ago?"

I made a mistake. I should have left him with the merchant.

"But why then are we going to the green hills? You have been cheated, Master."

"Why don't you ask your friend Ali of nowhere?" I cannot contain myself any longer.

"Oh, that will be difficult. He died many years ago. They say he was so strong that the dragon at the gates of the mountain had no choice but to let him enter, but only after four days and four nights of battle."

"Four nights of battle between your Ali and a dragon? What nonsense! I have had enough of these mountains already. I don't want to hear another—"

"No, no, Master, see this." He runs in front of me and takes a book from his dirty little sack.

Legendary Legends of the Central World.

After flipping through the pages, he hands me the book, ignoring my reluctance.

Legend says that only a true seeker can find the Mountains of Templetron. The one who does, must conquer the dragon at the gates before reaching the summit. There, he will find the King of Templetron who will grant him whatever he desires. The last known man to reach the summit was the Ali of Prusse. Because of his extraordinary strength, he was able to defeat the dragon after four entire nights of intense battle. What desire of the Ali was fulfilled, remains unknown.

"I am looking for directions, not a child's story." I hand the book back to him.

"Wait, Master... look here," he does not move out of my way.

"This legend is written by Mr Edgar Fligroin who lives in the village of Stonegis. This symbol is the emblem of Stonegis. We must find him, Master. He will surely know the way to the mountains."

"Elar, I don't have time to waste. The green hills are the only thing close to a mountain—"

"Master, the green hills cannot be the mighty Mountains of Templetron!"

Quite brave he is, for a servant.

"If they were, everyone would go there. And look at them, which dragon of any worth would be willing to protect those tiny hills?"

He makes a reasonable argument. They are mere mounds, a lazy attempt that nature seems to have abandoned.

"Master Ned-Har was right," he mumbles to himself.

"I'm sorry? I heard that."

"Master Ned-Har said, 'Elar, serve him well. He needs you. And don't tell him I said this.'"

"And you believe that?"

"I believe and accept everything my masters tell me."

"Yet he told you not to tell me."

"I didn't think of that," he mumbles. His face begins to shrink. He could tear up at any moment, and I am happy with that so long as he does it quietly. "I won't tell him. Just. Be. Quiet."

Elar

The air is finally beginning to change to that beautiful scent of the countryside. The closely packed brick houses have given way to timbered ones, scattered in the vast green landscape. I am so excited! I cannot believe it. A new master and a journey to the mightiest of mighty Mountains of Templetron. All in one day? My skin is tingling! If someone told me this yesterday, I would call them a lunatic. A madman. Aah! The meadows, and the river gurgling through, whispering to the rocks on the way. I know what it feels like, so much to say, such little time.

I walk along the river, listening to its every sound. The grass is up to my knees, gently tickling my legs. This is the first time I have walked here without a weight on my back. A yellow butterfly flutters around my face, rejoicing with me. Fish jump up from the water, swirl around and dive back in. The birds chirp and sing, and the tulips dance to their tune. All of them celebrating my new life. There are almost no people. Only a few peasants make their way to the fair with their hapless, overloaded donkeys. If only I could tell them how it feels to walk without a burden.

Not even a single cow is grazing. Even the vineyards are empty. I ask Master if he would like to bathe in the river, for I want to jump into it, again and again.

But he does not reply. I ask him if he is hungry. Still, he says nothing. I tell him the secret ingredient of the chicken broth. But he does not seem to hear me. I trot behind him, nonetheless. I wonder why he covers his head, why he always looks at the ground, not at the river, not at the tulips, not at the birds. He does not even look back to see if I am following. I could try to catch a rabbit or take a nap and he would not notice.

After walking for a few hours, we move away from the windy river and begin our approach to the village of Stonegis. We are now surrounded by fields of wheat. There is wheat and more wheat. The sky is not as clear. The air is very still. It must have rained just a little, for I smell wet earth, which makes it hard to breathe. The smell does funny things to my nose. And the dust makes me sneeze. In the distance, I see the arched entry to Stonegis, and nervousness replaces my excitement. We must find Mr. Fligroin. Please, Mother. Please. I need to find him.

I spot a farmer working in the fields as we pass through the arch. The village is walled on either side by wooden stakes. I run ahead of Master. I see no one, and my heart beats faster. I stop at the mill, but it is closed. Only ploughs lie inside the little church. The priest's house is locked. The stable is empty of horses. And it strikes me. It is the first day of the fair, after all. Mr. Fligroin may have gone there. I look around quickly, not knowing what to do. Master will be upset. I should have asked for Mr. Fligroin at the fair.

Surely, someone there would know such a famous man. I could have turned back instead of making Master walk all this way. What if he punishes me? No. No. Please be here, Mr. Fligroin. I run back towards the farmer as fast as I can.

SNEEZE. "Kind… kind sir, we travel from Corcusia. Looking for a man, a very famous man. You must know where I can find him. Please tell me where I can find him. Please."

"What is his name?"

The farmer is trying to calm me. At least, that is what I think. "Mr. Fligroin. Mr. Edgar Fligroin." I hurriedly take out the book.

"MISTER Fligroin?" He spits on the field, seemingly unhappy with my question. "That man can help nobody." The farmer waves his hand, dismissing me.

"No, kind sir, you don't understand." I show him the book of legends, not quite sure if he can read it.

"Don't blame me then," he sniggers. "Mr. Fligroin!" he mutters under his breath and gives me directions to an inn. Thank God! I can breathe again. The sun is setting, so I hurry back onto the path. Master has continued walking. I wonder where he is going. The sneezing plagues me. The poor farmer has to inhale dust all day long. Perhaps that's why he was irritated.

"Master, we must go to the village well. We will find Mr Fligroin at the inn," I say proudly.

He doesn't blink.

We pass the mill, the church, the priest's house and the stables before reaching the well at the centre of the village. On one side of it is the grain house, on the other, a small area that appears to be the blacksmith's shop, and a shed filled with many empty carts. I see stone dwellings just ahead of us and charge towards the only one with a lamp burning outside.

The innkeeper looks very happy to see me. "Kind sir, I look for—SNEEZE. "Sorry, for Mr. Fligroin."

"MISTER Fligroin?" he asks suspiciously, then points towards a dark corner and yells, "Fligroin, someone is here to see you."

I run past the empty chairs and the scattered tables. He is a famous man who must know many more legends. His back is towards me. He is wearing a tattered hat. I stop and smile widely at Master who makes his way towards Mr. Fligroin, and I follow behind him.

Mr. Fligroin appears middle-aged. From under his hat, grey hair falls over the shoulders of his threadbare coat. He is drinking ale while staring into a candle, which illuminates a giant spider web on the wall. As Master approaches him, he pulls his collar over his face and slowly raises his shoulders.

"Two days... you will have your money in two days," he slurs.

He owes Master money?

Master turns, shakes his head at me, and walks towards the door.

I am so confused. Why is Master leaving? We need Mr. Fligroin's help! "Mr. Fligroin…" I nervously call his name. He looks at me with questioning eyes nearly hidden under drooping lids. He reminds me of the hyena in the legend of— SNEEZE.

He seems quite upset. What famous man wouldn't be if a servant sneezed in his face?

"I am so sorry, kind Mr. Fligroin. I am Elar of Corcusia, servant to Andahar of… of…" I don't know where Master is from. "It is an honour to meet you, Mr. Fligroin—"

"What are you on about, boy?"

"We need your help."

Mr. Fligroin's shoulders begin to relax.

"We are here to discover from you, kind sir, the way to the Mountains of Templetron. My master must…" I place the book before him.

"Aaaah…" he says, and a wicked smile appears on his face. A cave hyena, smiling. His stinking mouth, with teeth that are dark yellow, even red in places, makes me take a step back.

"I can help you men, but I am leaving now. I will be back here after… umm… four days or forty. I know not." He strokes his patchy beard.

That is strange. I could imagine someone saying four days or five, thirty-five days or forty. But four or forty? "No, no, kind sir, we have travelled all the way from Corcusia!" I am on my knees.

"Too bad for you, Elar of wherever it is you come from. I cannot change my—"

"My master has gold coins," I quickly add.

The hyena's eyes light up.

"Hmmmm," he murmurs without blinking. "I am not a man looking for money, but since you are a sincere servant, I will tell you what you need to know. But for that, you will have to come with me, for it is my time to leave here."

He takes a large gulp of ale and stands up eagerly.

THANK YOU, MOTHER. I look up and close my eyes.

"Fligroin, don't you dare leave this place without…" The innkeeper's voice trails off as I run out to find Master, who has already begun walking ahead.

"Master, Master!" SNEEZE. "I did it, Master!"

"Now what have you done?" Master turns and looks at me with squinted eyes.

"I did it, I did it! Mr. Fligroin has agreed to help us and has kindly invited us to his—"

"Don't be a child. I will not waste time with this drunkard. Enough already."

I cannot understand. I had to beg Mr. Fligroin, and now he has agreed. And was Master about to leave me? "But Master—"

"Are we ready to go?" Mr. Fligroin calls from behind.

"Yes, yes, kind sir, we are ready," I add without looking at Master.

Master frowns and shakes his head ever so slightly.

"It's this way then," he points to an alley behind the inn. "Follow me, you may lodge at my house as you have travelled so far and… such important matters to discuss."

"And Mr. Fligroin, will you tell me all the legends you know?" I run to him.

He looks repulsed at first, but when his gaze meets Master's, he breaks into that wicked smile.

"Of course, boy! Lots of legends for you."

If he didn't look like the hyena, I would be completely sure that Mr. Fligroin was a nice man.

The sky is clear, but the night is cold. Only the crickets are out and about. For so many years, their song has lulled me to sleep. I wonder how they make that sound. Mr. Fligroin carries a lamp and I follow him closely. I must not lose him. I turn back to be certain Master is following. We make our way through the tight alley lined with small houses built of manure and straw. At the end of the alley, we cross a small bridge over a stream and find ourselves in the wheat fields once again. My eyes leak and my sneezing becomes more intense. After walking a short distance, we arrive at a hut near the village walls.

Mr. Fligroin uses all his strength to lift a small door as he gestures to us to enter. His smile scares me, but Master is a strong man. No harm will come to us. Perhaps Master is a little too strong. He finds it difficult to fit his shoulders through the door.

As we enter, I tread carefully amidst dirty clothes, empty jugs, and other things thrown about. Master seems unbothered. He picks up a sickle lying near the entrance and keeps it with him as he sits on a squeaky chair near a little pit in the middle of the room. I sit facing him on a damp mattress, which would have been much nicer if it did not smell of Mr. Fligroin.

Master does not look happy. What if he punishes me? No, no he will not. He is a kind man.

"Take this, boy. It will keep you warm." Mr. Fligroin hands me one of the jugs, then clumsily tries to light a fire in the pit.

The drink is horrendous. Bitter. I wish I had not taken such a big gulp. I try to warn Master, but he takes a few sips upon the urging of Mr. Fligroin.

Mr. Fligroin finally manages to light the fire and sits on a frayed rug. He hugs his knees and sways from side to side. "Where did you say you are from?"

"The Mountains of Templetron, that's where we need to go," Master replies abruptly.

SNEEZE. Perhaps he is a little harsh with Mr. Fligroin.

"Of course, which man wouldn't want his desires fulfilled?" he says, bobbing his head.

I feel dizzy and put my head down.

"Look, Fligroin—" Master puts down his jug.

"Can I offer you some porridge?" Mr. Fligroin interrupts.

I definitely do not want his porridge. I am scared to think how it must taste.

"No, I don't want any of your —"

"Oh, is it something else you prefer?"

I feel funny, my eyes are closing.

"Look, Fligroin, all we need to know is…" Master's voice trails off.

Andahar

Narcia looks... I don't know the right word. Divine? She wears a soft, cream-coloured sleeveless gown that flows to her ankles. It is a little loose, for it belongs to her mother, as is the tradition. A girdle of pink roses and violets is around her waist, and the same flowers with myrtle leaves brought by Ned-Har, form the little tiara on her head. A silver pin holds some of her golden brown hair, while the rest frames her beautiful face, flushed with a warm glow. Her jasmine scent fills the room.

Draped over my tunic, I wear a heavy, deep maroon robe embroidered with golden leaves, as the occasion demands. This is the most special day of my life. Only a few people are present: Narcia's parents, two of her friends, the physician and Ned-Har. Her mother has prepared smoked lamb pie and a flat cake of red apples, drizzled with honey and pistachios. Grape juice is flowing freely. Today we will exchange rings.

We sit with the priest who calculates the auspicious day for our wedding ceremony, based on the stars. Ned-Har prompts him to give us the soonest day possible. I think he may have slipped him a coin. Ned-Har holds my hand, and I notice a slight dampness in his eyes. It is the happiest day of our lives. I wonder why Rolanha is not here. He should be here soon.

Narcia and I are made to play the customary game of fishing the rings from a pot of milk sprinkled with red rose petals. Tradition dictates that whoever finds their partner's ring first, wins and can ask for anything they desire. I am desperately running my fingers through the milk, but all I find are petals. Narcia pinches my hand repeatedly, forcing me to pull it out each time. She giggles. She is glowing. I want to lose the game and give her everything she desires. But no, not so easily! Ned-Har cheers me on, while her friends and family cheer for her. Where is Rolanha when I need him!

The door is thrown open. Five of the king's guards enter, while two more stand sentinel at the door. One of them grips Narcia's arm. Her mother screams. I dart up and slam the guard into the wall, knocking him unconscious. How dare he? As I am about to turn, enraged and confused, I hear a loud thud and fall to the ground. My head is ringing, I have been hit by—Rolanha? My hands are being tied. Narcia's tiara is on the floor, and the guards are stamping over it as they drag her away. I fight hard to keep my eyes open. A pool of blood surrounds me.

I wake up gasping for air, my heart palpitating. Water drips on my face through a hole in the roof. I am tied up. My chair has fallen to the side. Elar is unconscious beside the firepit, his jug tipped over. Fligroin! I frantically look for my sack, but it is missing. I quickly break free and spring to my feet, my ears still ringing from the nightmare. I see Fligroin sitting at the doorway, my sack and the gold beside him. He holds something in his hand… the box! I charge towards him and snatch my things. Before he can say anything, I kick him in his stomach. He lies on the ground coughing wildly, and I lift him by his neck.

"Andahar, listen to me, please. You must listen to me," he says hoarsely as I hold him against the wall, his feet dangling in the air.

"You dishonourable pest!" I scream in his face. "You drugged me and tried to steal from me!" I tighten my grip around his neck.

"Please… please…"

"MASTER, he will die! Please, put him down!" Elar shouts from behind.

Fligroin is choking, his face turning red. Just a little tighter, and I will snap his neck.

"Master, PLEASE MASTER!"

Elar holds my arm, but I don't relent. My body trembles with rage. I will kill this man.

"MASTER!" Elar screams, almost hanging by my arm.

Just as I am about to snap his neck, I gain control of myself and throw him to the ground. He desperately gasps for air while Elar dashes to fetch water.

"You… you don't understand," Fligroin tries to speak. His eyes are bloodshot.

"Mr. Fligroin, please—have this." Elar holds his head, helping him sip the water.

"Yes, I was about to steal your gold and—" the coughing continues, "this box that you carry, until I saw the symbol on it," Fligroin gasps for air.

"Don't listen to this man, Elar! Your silly trust in his stories has got us into this mess. This is just another story. You can choose to stay here if you like. I am done." I pick up the box and the pouch of gold and put them into my sack.

"Believe what you must but tell me one thing—" he pauses to cough. "Do you think I would be sitting here, waiting for you to wake up when I had already managed to get the gold? I could start a new life!"

"That's true, Master." Elar nods vigorously. "Why would he sit there with the box in his hand and wait for us to wake up? He surely doesn't think he can fight you."

I do not believe this.

"Please tell me, where did you get this box?" Fligroin asks impatiently.

"No more games, Fligroin." I wag my finger in his face. "I will not let you go this time!"

"Master, please…"

"Do you have the key?" Fligroin persists, not bothered in the least.

What key?

"Andahar, please look at the box," he continues to insist.

Reluctantly, I remove the box from my sack and hold it tightly.

"Look at this symbol. It is an ancient emblem, the significance of which very few people understand. And the unearthly glow. Look at it."

I try hard not to admit but the glow is strangely enchanting.

"Whatever is inside this box, it—"

He rattles off in a language I do not understand while staring at me wide-eyed, "Tell me, Andahar, do you have the key?"

"Look, Fligroin, this box was entrusted to me by my brother, a merchant in exotic goods. He has spent ten years looking for this object. All I know is that I must deliver it to the King of Templetron." I carefully put the box into its velvet cover before placing it in my sack.

"Andahar, try to understand what I am saying, whatever this box contains is priceless," he pleads.

"I care not what it carries, nor how it came about. I must deliver the box and return to the ship. So, if you know how to reach the Mountains of Templetron, this is your last chance to tell me."

"Master, please," Elar says, holding my arm.

"Fulfilling all he can desire has been man's objective since the beginning of time," Fligroin says. "According to the legend, the Mountains of Templetron contain the essence and energy of a great sage who attained realisation there. It is said that this sage became an omniscient and omnipotent being, the human embodiment of the divine. He could not only manifest anything but also grant the wishes of a true and worthy recipient."

Fligroin appears to be a completely different man now, not even a shade of the scoundrel we met at the inn. For the first time, I notice his striking blue eyes.

"Many years ago, I met that sage. He arrived in Corcusia, a wandering monk. In those days, I was an apprentice to a craftsman, having failed to learn a trade from both a blacksmith and a bread maker. It was an ordinary, boring day, and I wandered into the square for a stroll after my mid-day meal. As I made my way back to the shop, I saw a monk walking in the opposite direction. Our eyes met. He smiled at me ever so gently. There was an unusual radiance on his face. I was absolutely mesmerised by his charisma, completely lost in his presence, till I was jolted by the shrill voice of a woman calling out to him. She ran up from behind and bent down in front of him, saying all she sought were his blessings. He smiled humbly, and as he was about to continue on his way, she began to sob.

"'Oh, learned one, my daughter is birthing a child, but the physician says that both she and the child may die. Is it true?'

"I found it amusing but looked to see what the monk could possibly know about childbirth.

"'They will live,' he said with authority, before beginning to walk ahead.

"'Really? They will live?' She stopped him again.

"He smiled at her and said, 'It will be her fourth child. You will be a grandmother again soon. Worry not.' And he walked briskly ahead.

"She wailed, 'You are right! It is her fourth child. Thank you, oh Sage. Thank you!' She got up smiling and wiped away her tears. Seeing me stare, she said, 'He knows it all.'

"'Does he not know you?' I asked. How else would he have known it was the fourth child?

"'No, we meet for the first time, but from his appearance, I knew he was a learned and gifted being. You must ask for his blessings.'"

Elar gasps.

"I was astounded by the event and sure this monk must be adept in the art of magic. I ran to him and fell to his feet.

"'Please, please, teach me,' I begged.

"'You are not ready,' he said and continued to walk.

"'Then please, let me be in your service,' I pleaded, following him.

"'It is not an easy path,' he said without looking at me.

"'I will do whatever you say.'

"He paused and looked at me for just a second before agreeing.

"Instead of returning to the craftsman, I started in the monk's service. I helped him find a place in the countryside far from the noise and din, as he desired to spend time in quiet contemplation. He did not have the look of a monk who had ever needed to beg, and although I cooked for him, I was instructed that my every meal must come only from alms. It was hard. People were harsh, even abusive, but I had no choice. He said it was part of my training, for my ego needed tempering. Despite the difficult days, when I returned to him, everything felt fine. He had a powerful but extraordinarily soothing air about him. It was only after a few months that he began imparting knowledge to me." Fligroin continues his tale, staring into the dwindling fire.

"He was a great and noble teacher, wise and extremely kind. His only concern was helping me find my own truth. He overlooked my negative traits, saying that with time and effort, I would learn to overcome them. He used to say that magic was only ever the result of finding oneself. But I was young and foolish. Deep down, I wanted to learn the art so I could become strong, wealthy, and invincible. I did not realise that I was asking the monk for a mortal firefly when he was offering me the undying sun. After a lot of practice, I began to hone my abilities, especially the power of intuition. Soon enough, with my newfound skills and fast-growing ego, I began to hate the rigorous and boring life. My ignorance led me to question myself. Why did I need to wake up before sunrise and bathe in the river, even in the freezing winter? Why did I have to bow down and thank the sun, the stones, the animals, and every other thing? I was no longer an ordinary person. I didn't need to beg worthless people for food. I could use my new skills to make a fortune. I had endured enough, and the time had come to enjoy it. Thoughts of running away began to emerge. The sage continued to behave towards me as he always did, like a father, gentle but firm, loving but strict. The night before I planned to escape, he stayed with me a little longer than usual.

"'Edgar, the more you move away from yourself, the more you will lose in life. But remember, it is never too late.'" Fligroin pauses. His eyes well up.

"I did not understand what he meant and did not bother to ask. Much later, it struck me that he knew I was planning to run away. And I did, the next day. Back into the tempting land of Corcusia. Tired of the rigours I had faced, I decided to use my skills to make a quick fortune. Success came through gambling, betting and even fortune-telling. As the money came in, I used it to gratify my senses, whether through women, liquor or other substances that were plentiful during the trading season. As with all empty satisfaction, nothing was enough. More women, different liquor, more exotic substances, and the bad company that comes with them. Little did I know that the more I was consumed by pride, the more I was blinded. The more blind I became, the less I could hear the voice the sage had taught me to listen to. With the passage of time, I became addicted and slowly, slowly lost my gifts. The most dangerous addiction I had acquired was that of having an easy life, and without my gifts, I soon fell into a vicious trap of debt.

"Like the child who stubbornly writes off his parents as fools who know nothing of life and walks down the path his parents beg him to avoid. Like the child who one day stands exactly where his parents stood, trying his hardest to save his own stubborn progeny from years of misery, like that child, I ignored the monk and his teachings, only to realise later what my immaturity had cost me. I travelled across the lands in search of him once again, hearing stories of his greatness, his kindness, and sometimes, of the miracles he had performed. During this search, I heard scarce and scattered stories about the Ali of Prusse, the dragon, and the Mountains of Templetron. I searched and searched but found no sign of him, and I was forced to accept that I had run away from the greatest blessing I could have ever received." He pauses to sip some water.

"Much later, a traveller came searching for me, a man who claimed to be compiling a book on the legends of the central world. How he found me, I know not. But he said he gathered I was the man who could tell him about the Legend of the Mountains of Templetron. He said I would receive credit for the story. After a lot of cajoling, I agreed to tell him what I knew, hoping that somewhere, someone who knew about the sage would knock at my door. But in all these years, I have only been visited by ignorant and mischievous people seeking the way to the mountains.

"It is said that it takes immense faith, courage, and perseverance to reach the mountains, and that only a truly worthy person will manage to battle his way to the summit after surmounting the harshest trials."

I interrupt him. "Fligroin, I only need to know the way."

"Unfortunately, all I know is that one must travel through the Forest of Santia to the mystical Lake Fonlius. It is said that upon bathing in the near freezing water at midnight, one will be welcomed by mermaids who are believed to have the key to the journey ahead. But you must enter the lake at—"

"The Forest of Santia?" Elar asks, his eyes wide open.

"Fligroin, I would like to discard everything you have said, but..." I pause, wondering if this is just another trick.

"But Mr. Fligroin, the Forest of Santia is..." Elar mumbles.

"Please, if you see him on this journey, tell him all I ask is his forgiveness and his blessings so I can redeem myself." Fligroin is choking on his words.

"Mr. Fligroin. The Forest of—"

"What is it, Elar?" I ask, irritated.

"Master, you don't understand. The Forest of Santia is famed across our lands, for it is said to be cursed. For reasons unknown, no one who ventures into this forest comes back alive."

"One must travel through this forest at night," Fligroin says casually. "The sage once told me that sometimes, what light cannot give you, darkness can. Often, it is the darkness in your life that sets you on your true path. It is the darkness, that lights your way. The only way to traverse the Forest of Santia is in darkness."

"But Mr. Fligroin—"

"Oh, listen to me first, boy." Fligroin waves a hand at Elar. "Remember three things: First, under no circumstances must you travel during daylight. Second, follow the brightest path, but do not touch anything. Third, the brighter it is, the more poisonous."

"The brighter what is? You said we must follow the brightest path and now you say it is the most poisonous?" Elar tugs at his cloak like an annoying little child.

Before long, I shake Fligroin's hand and Elar hugs him as we set out for the Forest of Santia with the first rays of sunshine.

Elar

By the time we enter the forest, it is nightfall. It would be pitch dark if not for the little dots scattered all across the ground. Some emit a soft yellow light, while others, orange, blue and green. As we get closer, I can see that the dots of light are creatures, a variety of tiny organisms, some so small you wouldn't see them if it were not for their light. Innumerable of them, glowing a dull silver, are stuck to the narrow tree trunks as they rise into the sky. There seems to be only one kind of tree in this forest. Thankfully, they are a short distance apart, giving us enough space to walk between them. Master carefully chooses the most brightly lit path.

"Elar, you must not step on them. Even the slightest touch and you will be dead."

"Yes, Master."

The lights from the tiny creatures on the forest floor and the tree trunks merge to form a spectacular radiance. "Master," I whisper. He turns back immediately. "Mr. Fligroin made it sound so scary, but it isn't all that bad. Just a few insects that may be quite poisonous, but nothing more than that."

Suddenly, what sounds like an owl hoots, and I jump closer to Master. Before I can blink, I hear hissing from not too far away. I see the bright red light of a thick snake with green eyes. It flickers its brown tongue for a moment, then hisses louder. The head of another aggressively hissing snake becomes visible. The patterns across its skin make it look brighter than the first one, but it emits a dull orange light. There is a chilling silence, then they leap into the air, intertwine their bodies, and attack each other. *Now* my hair stand on end. Master looks at me and smiles to himself before moving ahead. I stay close to him. Curious, I turn around. The red snake is swallowing the orange one. UGH! I almost vomit.

As we make our way ahead, we encounter more animals. A white mouse with a dull blue light peeps from a hole in the ground. A giant squirrel with a soft white light hangs from a tree. A green-eyed toad with a bright blue light merrily jumps across our path and nearly lands on my feet. I no longer think of the lights as pleasing. Just then, a big beautiful butterfly with a soft bronze hue flutters above Master's head. He pauses and bends down slightly, while the butterfly flies ahead, only to get entangled in a huge spider web made visible by its own light. A bright green spider crawls towards it, while it tries hard to disentangle itself. I want to yank it out, but Master scolds me. There are moths and lizards aplenty. On our path ahead, we see many more snakes—black ones glowing with red spots, light green ones with golden spots, blue ones with silver. Snakes. I hate them.

Although their colouring is most elegant, I don't have the stomach to appreciate them. The brightest of all lights is emitted by succulent giant berries that glitter in shades of purple as they hang from wild shrubs. Never have I seen such inviting fruit. Master only needs to look at me, and I keep my distance from them.

"We must get to the stones before sunrise," Master says, almost inaudibly. "According to Fligroin, it is the only safe place during the day." He moves quickly but cautiously. The trees begin to give way to gigantic rock formations. While most are shaped like pillars, some are flat like a wall. A few shapes are rather unique, like the ones resembling men in capes who appear to be deep in conversation. Or the giant ball precariously held up by two tall pillars. I feel like a dwarf walking through them. They are overbearing. There is something mysterious and at the same time, majestic about them. The formations do not have any light of their own apart from the small yellow patches of dully lit moss on their surface. They reflect the silver light emitted by the few trees around. After travelling through the rather radiant path, these dimly lit surroundings are a relief. Master finds a small opening, a kind of cave at the base of a tall rock, big enough for both of us to rest. He goes in first, and after a few moments, asks me to join. I sit inside the cave, while Master sits at the entrance. Soon, the sun rises, and the forest changes. Master does not allow me to come close to the opening, but I can see in the distance that none of the lights that guided our path are visible now. The forest appears deceptively serene and pleasant, which explains why it has earned such a deadly reputation. I look at Master, who seems to have worn the same expression since the moment I met him, betraying not a trace of fear. I allow myself to close my eyes, knowing he is there to protect me.

*

"Elar, it is time to leave." I feel a nudge. "Elar, wake up!" I sit up immediately to find that it is dark outside. "We must leave now." Master steps out and inspects the area before gesturing me to follow.

"Yes, Master." I pick up my sack and groggily follow as he makes his way down, lending me a hand. An eerie feeling descends upon me as I see the forest lit up in the distance. We walk down the path from the cave and come upon an area where the forest floor is dense with bright lights. It requires much more care to walk. The trees are now thicker and have gigantic roots that swell up and crisscross to form a huge web. The mammoth roots are even higher than Master's head. Thankfully, only a few red dots of light are scattered across them. Master tells me to wait while he carefully climbs up a root and peers over on the other side. He then reaches for my hand and pulls me up. It will be a big jump down, but thankfully, no light glitters on the ground. The small dark area is barely lit. My relief is short lived as I see the narrow pathway that winds upwards into a tight space between two giant pillars standing very close together. They are entirely covered in moss that is glowing bright yellow. I look at Master who seems completely focused on the task ahead.

"I will go first," he says. He jumps down and tells me to follow.

I land on my feet and smile widely at him. He turns and sighs. The brightly lit yellow rocks look even more imposing, the path between them even narrower. Suddenly, I hear a rustling behind me. Master turns and freezes. I try to ignore the noise, but the frown on his face does not let me. More rustling.

"Elar…" he says softly. "When I tell you, jump as far right as you can."

"What is… behind me, Master?" My voice quivers and my legs begin to tremble.

For a moment, there is a creepy silence.

"NOW!" he screams, and I jump as far as I can, falling to the ground.

A giant lizard leaps up and lands just where I was standing moments ago. It is now face to face with Master. My heart races. The lizard is stone-coloured, long, with strong bowed legs and a muscular tail. Master tries to dodge it, but it unfurls its long, slithery tongue and catches him by the foot, before yanking him from him side to side. Master tries hard to kick it off but is unsuccessful. It pulls him closer with one swift move and bites into his leg. Screaming, Master kicks it hard in the face. Startled, the lizard moves its head away, momentarily letting go of his leg. Then it leaps onto Master, who manages to catch it by its jaws. The lizard unfurls its slimy tongue and wraps it around Master's neck. I move closer and throw large stones at the creature, but it tosses me aside with its tail. It is trying to choke Master, but he continues to pull its jaws wider and wider. It begins to shriek and loses its hold on Master's neck. Its tongue slaps about frantically. Master screams even louder than the lizard and pulls hard. There is a sharp squeal, and all goes quiet. He throws the lizard off his body.

I rush to him. "Master, are you fine? I didn't know what to—" he sits up and raises a hand before grasping his thigh.

"Master, it was not emitting any light. It was probably not poisonous. You should be fine." He looks at me and lifts his hand from his thigh. The wound is deep. It looks horrible. If his thigh were any smaller, the lizard would have severed it.

"But… it sure had sharp teeth," I gulp.

"You think so, Elar?"

I try to help him stand, but he pushes me away.

"Master, please allow me to—"

"Ssssh! Do you hear that?"

"Another one?" This time, I freeze completely.

"No, the singing? Can you hear it? It's coming from there." Master limps up the path leading to the narrow opening between the giant rocks. As I follow him, I hear it too. "Master, let me lead the way. It is too narrow, and your leg is—"

"Quiet, Elar. You will do no such thing. You will wait for me to get across before starting."

"But Master…"

He removes the sack from his back and holds it beside him as he takes small sideways steps between the rocks. Blood drips from his leg, but he continues unbothered and with utmost concentration. I heave a huge sigh of relief once he crosses over successfully. I walk through the opening carefully but comfortably, keeping my hands beside me as instructed. As I reach Master, the singing becomes louder, and the air cooler. The forest becomes denser, the light-emitting beings, rarer. We move between tall trees, now growing closer. Beyond them, I see a light blue hue rising in the sky. The ground begins to slope downward, aiding our tired bodies.

I am awe struck.

Lake Fonlius. A huge body of shimmering turquoise water, as if lit up magically in the dark night. The water glistens as though adorned with a multitude of tiny diamonds that sparkle gleefully on its surface. The slight movement of the shy waves adds to the mysterious charm. Mist dances over the lake while the colour of the brilliant water is reflected off the majestic trees who stand guard. As we go closer to the lake, we enter the mist. It is cold now. Really cold. I wrap my arms around myself in a futile attempt to keep warm.

We see them clearly now. The mermaids. Never have I seen a sight so angelic. Some of them are swimming, others, playing together, diving in and out of the water, and singing the most alluring songs. Their luscious, long, wet hair ranges from a magical walnut brown to deep gold. They have a dewy, radiant complexion which is flawless. Their bodies are well endowed, with skin that appears soft and supple. Every one of them has a graceful tail that tapers into a fin marked by dazzling scales, glittering in colours I know not how to name— metallic green, deep blue, light yellow, and an exquisite bronze. The air is filled with a fragrance that makes me light-headed. They call my name, beckoning me to them. I cannot resist.

One mermaid lies atop a rock on a small island in the centre of the lake. She looks at me teasingly, fluttering her eyelashes and mesmerising me with her hypnotic gaze. Her face rests on her arm while her sweet lips part just enough as she sings my name, stroking her hair and gesturing me to come to her. Her dark brown skin glimmers with droplets of water, and she gently flaps her golden fin most invitingly. I desire nothing but her embrace, her touch, her kiss.

"Elar…"

"Elar!" Master shouts as he begins to disrobe. His back is severely marked. "Sorry, Master— it is too cold, Master. You will die if you enter the water." My teeth chatter as I try hard to fight the lightness in my head and the tingling warmth I get from looking at that mermaid.

"It is nearly midnight," Master says. "If there is any truth in what Fligroin said, this is the only way we will find our way to the mountains. Keep this safe." He hands me his sack and moves to the edge of the water. "Elar, you are not to enter the water under any circumstances."

The way she calls my name. It melts my heart. I must go to her. We must be complete. All my life…

"ELAR! Did you hear me?" Master's voice pulls me back to my senses.

"Yes, sire." I cover my ears, but I can still hear her. She begs me. I close my eyes to keep her out and open them upon hearing Master screaming as he enters the water. He begins swimming towards the centre of the lake. The singing gets louder. It is almost deafening. The air, the song, the mermaids, it all makes me dizzier than I have ever been.

As Master reaches the centre of the lake, a short distance from the island, the music stops. The mermaids no longer call my name. The breeze is gone.

The lake is pitch black, reflecting an enormous orange moon in its still waters. I don't see them anymore. It has become colder. I cannot take it any longer. I fall to my knees and hug them close. Something moves under the water. It is red. Master has been sucked in.

Andahar

"MASTER... MASTER!"

My body is burning.

"Master, please wake up... Master, please be well!"

"Is he alright?" I ask anxiously.

"Is who alright? What are you talking about, Master?"

Too many questions. I open my eyes to see Elar blocking the sun. My head is in his lap.

"All I can see in the four directions is sand! Sand, sand, sand and sand," he says, pointing.

"A desert? How did we get here?" I try to adjust my eyes to the blinding brightness.

"Master, I have not a clue! I woke up with sand in my clothes and a burning backside! I looked around. I was so frightened. Thankfully, I saw you lying here and have been trying to wake you up ever since."

I cannot bear the sound of his voice. A heaviness spreads across my body. I am more exhausted than I have ever been.

"What happened at the lake?" he asks. Finally, a useful question.

"Oh yes! The lake! The mermaids and... and that..." I begin to remember through the fogginess of my mind.

"It was quite cold, Master. Someone with less strength than mine would have surely died." The boy puffs his chest a little.

"What did you see from the banks?"

"Not much." He bites his nails.

"Not much?"

"After it all went dark, I could see the reflection of the moon in the water. Master, it was orange! I have never seen anything like that before. Very spooky. Suddenly, I saw a light. A red light moving swiftly towards you, and the next minute, you were gone! After that... I don't remember anything." He pauses. "How did we get here, Master?"

"The water was cold. The river in the Blue Mountains was child's play compared to this—"

"The Blue Mountains? Is that where you are from, Master?"

I ignore his meaningless question. "I remember screaming to get my blood going. Those mermaids got louder and louder as they drew me to the centre of the lake." I sit up. Trying to think hard. But the sun drains the life from me. The sand on my back burns.

"Master, could you hear them calling my name, too?"

"Your name?"

The mermaids called my name so loudly, he must be delusional.

"Yes, Master. They all did, especially the one with the golden fin. Now I remember, she came to me, and she was in love—"

"Elar, please!" I dismiss him and his stories. I try to remember, but my head is pounding.

"Really, Master, she showed me—"

"Elar. Not now. I am trying to remember, and you are not helping. So… As I… reached the centre of the lake, everything went silent. No calling. No singing. No mermaids. All was still. Then… I felt something entangle my body. I was completely caught in it and sucked under the water through the darkness. Fast, very fast. Suddenly, whatever it was that was gripping me, set me free. There was a moment of calm as I floated freely, my body no longer tangled. But I felt that I was not alone, that I was being watched. Then, in a flash, I was encircled by… Yes! Mermaids! But they were ugly. Not a shade of their earlier form. They completely surrounded me and were close, very close. These wicked looking mermaids snarled at me with their sinister fangs and almost pierced me with their sharp tails."

"Master, those mermaids couldn't harm anyone, trust me. Especially the one who took me to the other—"

Elar goes quiet as I stare at him.

"I thought they would kill me, but then they made way for something like a giant snake. 'Why are you here?' the snake spoke in a calm feminine voice.

She looked stately as she moved, her body, a dull white with a golden pattern all over. As she gracefully made her way towards me, the patterns kept changing and moving as if they had a mind of their own. Some kind of a smoky form danced above her head. It kept changing shape, it kept changing colour. All along the snake's form was a subtle glow. The mermaids bowed their heads and pointed their tails up as she stopped in front of me. 'You will die in less than half a minute. What do you seek?' she said while her hypnotic eyes peered into mine.

"'I seek the Mountains of Templetron,' I replied.

"'Many a man has come here, looking for the mountains, for the Realm of Desires Fulfilled. Most of them were seduced into entering these waters, but met a painful death not long after. It is our job to ensure that greed, hate, and selfish motives stay away from the Realm. And for that, you shall be tested. When you fail, your name will be added to the long list of men who have lost their lives in this lake.'

"Before I could completely understand what she said, I was blinded by a strong light. My body shook uncontrollably, and a strong current raged through me."

"You were stung?"

Elar gives me his wide-eyed look. "This is almost like a legend! Then what happened, Master?"

"I think... I can't remember anything more." My head is throbbing relentlessly.

"But Master, Mr. Fligroin said—"

"If I ever see Fligroin again, I will kill him. He forgot to tell us that I would be sucked into the water and nearly drown, or that the mermaids would turn into vicious creatures from hell. Or that I would be struck by a bolt of lightning—"

"Master!" he shrieks. "Your leg! It has healed!"

"What?"

"See, Master. You didn't die, and it appears we passed the test—"

"We? Did WE pass the test?"

"Yes, you did a little more than I did, but we are a team, are we not?" he chuckles.

A smile emerges on my face. A strange feeling. I don't remember the last time that happened. "Help me up and find some shade before we actually die this time."

Elar summons all his energy to lift my arm around his shoulder, only to sink into the sand.

"There you go, young man, there's teamwork for you!"

"Yes… sire," he says, trying not to fall.

Walking in the desert is a challenge, even with Elar supporting me. The continuous slipping and sinking into the hot sand takes every ounce of effort, and the sun feels like a fire-breathing dragon determined to burn us down. If the dragon guarding those mountains is anything like this, it will certainly be the end of us. The air is extremely dry, and from time to time, a strong gust of hot wind blows sand into our faces. It sticks to my parched lips and my teeth, which irritates me even more. But what bothers me most is the sight ahead of us: dune after dune, flowing into the distance, with no sign of shelter or shade. Elar does his best to help me. "Stop," I say. "Do you hear that?"

"Oh no, not again. Please, Master. Whatever it is, may it show mercy!"

"Listen quietly." From a distance, we hear men chattering and bells ringing discordantly.

"Master!" Elar screams a little too close to my ear. "A group of travellers is coming our way."

He helps me turn, and I see a caravan making its way down a dune. As they come closer, I notice five men dressed in loose fitting gowns, their faces covered with scarves. They wear oversized turbans on their heads. One of them is dressed differently. While the others wear grey gowns, his is slightly darker with silver designs on its long sleeves. The others wear a purple turban, but his is deep blue. He must be their leader. He rides in the middle, and his turban seems larger, with some sort of insignia at its centre. Big copper ornaments hang from the ears of the other four, while his seem to be of silver. They all wear rings on all their fingers. A riderless camel carries their belongings.

"Gentlemen," Elar bows his head and folds his hands as they approach us. "If you would permit my master and I to ride with you as we seek shelter, we would be very grateful and... and my master being the generous man that he is, will pay you in gold."

I give him that look, but the truth is, I would happily trade gold for water and a camel to ride on. The men silently exchange confused glances.

The caravan leader uncovers his face. A silver ring hangs between both his nostrils, and a thick silver band encircles his neck. He is a tall, well-built man. "Young man, gold or no gold, helping one in need is our duty." He speaks in an accent I do not recognise. "We are returning to our village. If you and your master can ride on one camel, you are welcome to join us."

I heave a sigh of relief, a feeling I did not imagine I would experience ever again.

"Thank you for your kindness, sir. We are deeply indebted," Elar says. He turns towards me and whispers, "I am not sure the camel will be happy with your weight, sire." I ignore him and nod at the caravan leader gratefully.

"Elar," I mutter, "Pray there will be no more surprises, or you will fight them yourself."

"Oh, don't worry, sire. None of these men will harm us... will they?"

He climbs onto the camel, then three of the men help me mount the hapless animal. As I am finally off my feet, I realise how tired I am. The rhythmic trudging of the camel lulls me to sleep amidst the sound of its bells and Elar's relentless chatter.

Andahar

I stand on barren land that stretches on endlessly. On either side of the slightly raised, obscure pathway, I see numerous little craters stained a deep yellow. Otherwise, the landscape is a desolate grey. In the distance, a volcano spews ash and molten lava. I cannot tell the time of day, for the sky is uniformly red. The air is thick with a pungent smell that makes it difficult to breathe. The ground trembles frequently, causing the stones to vibrate. Dead trees are scattered about, and I see a few pyres burning between them. The bleakness of the place is overpowering. My leg burns. I feel something trickling down. Blood. I look closer to find that I have been injured. An animal bite of some kind. Relatively deep. I notice a being overlooking the flames that rise from the pyres as the fire eats into the logs of wood. As I make my way towards this being, the ground shakes fiercely, throwing up gases, hissing while the volcano rumbles powerfully, spewing more ash. I do not see them, but I hear vultures screeching. Anger courses through my being.

"What is this place?" I ask the being whose cape matches the red of the sky. It has no feet and hovers a few inches above the ground. It turns, but its face is darkly shadowed by a hood. In that darkness, I see large yellow eyes and grey skin scaled with lines.

"This is the Realm of Justice Delivered, where punishment is meted out to sinners, where those of noble heart sacrifice the lives of evildoers to nature." It has the voice of a man, gruff and cold.

"How did I get here?"

"Those are the pyres of nefarious mortals who have been purged from humanity by men quite like yourself."

"What do you mean?"

"Andahar of the Blue Mountains, a great warrior, an honourable one. You are a special man to whom life has been excessively harsh."

And he disappears.

I look around and see him a little ahead, hovering between two craters that belch hot air.

"Your parents were taken away. Your brother became a cripple." His voice echoes over the hissing of the geysers as I watchfully make my way towards him. "Many a battle you fought and many a land you conquered for the king…"

Just as I am about to reach him, he vanishes again.

"The king who took everything from you," he whispers into my ear from behind.

I clench my fists.

"And left you with your greatest regret, is it not?"

I hear fingers snapping near my ears, and I am transported to a day long ago, to the Ceremony of Rings.

"Yes, it was the happiest day of your life," says the caped being.

I am standing in a corner of the room. I see Narcia looking magnificent in her gown, with flowers adorning her head and waist. I see myself, not a shade of the man I am today. I wear a maroon robe embroidered with golden leaves. My hair is neatly tied back. I concentrate deeply as I try to find the ring in the pot of milk. Narcia is pinching me. She laughs as she does it. Rose petals stick to my hand as I pull it out. Ned-Har cheers me on.

"Andahar," I rush to warn myself, "you must take her and run! Andahar!" I scream, but my former self does not hear me. "Narcia, leave! Now! You must leave!" She continues laughing.

I beg Ned-har, but he does not hear me either.

"NO! NO! You have to stop this! DO SOMETHING!" I scream at the caped creature standing behind me. The door flings open, and the king's guards enter.

"You know what happens next—" the creature says.

"NO! We must—" I hear fingers snapping again.

We are back at the volcano. "WHY DID YOU TAKE ME AWAY?" I fall to my knees, screaming.

"Everything was taken from you, but did you deserve it?" the creature whispers, as though slowly inserting a knife into my wounded heart.

"NO!" I scream, "All I ever did—"

"Was fulfil your duty? An evil man took it all away. And look at what has become of you."

I scream wildly and bang my fists on the ground until blood oozes from them.

"What if I told you that you could have the life you always desired, the life you truly deserve?" he asks, and the fingers snap again.

We are in a meadow. I see a charming cottage atop a small hill overlooking the countryside. I hear the voices of children laughing, and I run up the hill. Ned-Har is playing with three children, chasing them around. He is not crippled. He laughs loudly as he catches one of them and screams towards the house. "I caught the little pirate, Andahar. He's yours to punish now!" The boy giggles as Ned-Har tickles him.

The boy's hair is golden brown. He looks exactly like—

"Mother... Mother!" he screams, and I look towards the house with bated breath. Before I can see anything else, I hear the fingers snap again.

"No, please... please let me—" I beg the caped creature.

"You can have it, Andahar. You can have everything that should rightfully be yours. All you must do is—"

"I will do anything," I say. "Please!"

"Deliver a life."

"A life?"

"An evil life must be sacrificed so that balance is restored. Deliver the life, and Nature will bless you with all that is rightfully yours. Look what has become of you, living like a dead man, paying the price for the wicked deeds of another."

My resentment has never been greater.

"Do you not want it? Your life, your brother's ability to walk—"

"I do. I will do it. Tell me whom I must kill, and I will bring you his head."

The caped being vanishes, then reappears in the distance. He enters the mountain through an opening in the rocks. I hurry after him and find myself in a tunnel. A steep, stony pathway spirals up and opens into a narrow passage. The caped being stands at the far end.

He says, "In the cave beyond this veil is a greedy, selfish man who has stolen from many, leaving their families desperate and poor. This man has brought only misery and pain to the people around him. He is a treacherous cheat whose heart is filled with pride. Go in and kill him with the mace that can be wielded only by the one of noble heart." He points towards a curtain of a blackish light, waving gently.

I walk through it and find the man standing at the edge of the cave overlooking an enormous lake of lava. He turns towards me. I recognise him without knowing how. Grey hair falls from under his tattered hat, and his cloak is threadbare. His eyes are the same yellow as those of the caped being.

"Did they not find anyone better? A man so fallen himself?" he asks, baring his yellow teeth, which are stained red in places.

"Quiet!" I scream, thrashing him to the ground.

"You sent this man?" he yells. "He could not even save his own—"

The caped being's voice resounds in the cave. "He is a pest. Listen to the way he speaks, that drunken pride—"

"I said quiet!" I punch the man again, and he laughs. "You deserved every bit of what happened, and you, you were the cause of it." I knock him again. Blood flows from his nose, but he keeps smiling and staring at me with those yellow eyes as I dangle his head from the edge of the cave.

"Finish him, for the sake of mankind," the caped being prods. I pick up the mace as his voice grows louder and louder. "For your brother… for yourself, and most of all… for Narcia." Suddenly, the scent of jasmine fills the air. For a moment, the man's eyes turn blue, and in an instant, I know him. He is none other than Edgar Fligroin.

"Don't you want to wake up in her arms? How much longer must you suffer?" The caped being's voice blares in the cave. "Remember that you never trusted this man. Remember that he cheated you, as well. Finish him and take everything you ever deserved."

"NO!" I scream. "You lie! This is not the evil man. You are!" I turn swiftly, but before I can land the mace, the caped being drives a sword through my heart. I fall to the ground in numbing pain, and the creature vanishes. My vision blurs. I hear a buzzing sound. All goes dark, I no longer feel pain. There is no heaviness. There is a light, and I move towards it.

"I have spent centuries at the bottom of the lake, protecting this realm from the insatiable hunger of men." The light speaks to me in a voice much like that of the snake in Lake Fonlius. "Not many have come this far. It is easy to silence your conscience and forget what you truly stand for when the possibility of fulfilling your every desire is placed before you. In that moment of choice, even the mightiest can be rendered powerless. At that significant juncture, when you must choose between that which you desire and the price you are willing to pay for it, is the true test of one's character. You were shown a life and promised a world that was everything you have ever wanted. A life free from the deep pain you and your loved ones have suffered. But in that moment of choice, under the pressure of the greatest temptation, you saw beyond your sorrow. You saw the man you were meant to kill for who he really was, a man who suffers deeply, who seeks forgiveness and redemption. You were able to save yourself from committing an act which would have only taken you further away from where you needed to be."

The light continues, gently caressing my wounds. "Although you blame yourself and carry deep anger, although you believe you are a man of little worth, in the moment that mattered, you chose to see the truth. Mind you, Andahar, as you have throughout your life, you had free will even during your test. You could well have taken the man's life. It might even have seemed an insignificant price to pay for all you were promised in return, but you chose goodness over evil, light over darkness, virtue over vice. And for this, you have been rewarded with the key to your journey ahead. Use it wisely."

The scent of jasmine fills the air as serenity courses through my veins. I hear a whisper. *"See the meaning."*

I wake up to an unusual calmness. I am in a small room with walls made of mud bricks. It is dimly lit by an oil lamp that is placed in an alcove in the wall. A well polished metal plate hangs next to it. A mirror. The ceiling is flat and low. I lay on a straw mat. My head rests on a pillow stuffed with feathers. I see another mat at an arm's length. I am dressed in a loose gown of a cool and comfortable fabric.

I jump to my feet and look around frantically. I rummage through my sack, Elar's sack, under the mat, the pillow, but I cannot find them. My clothes are missing.

I dash out of the hut. It is nightfall. I look around to find a few more huts. They are identical, with a short ladder lying beside each of their entrances. I hear laughter coming from a well lit area not far away. I run towards it and find Elar sitting in a courtyard with five other men, all wearing gowns like mine with turbans on their heads. They laugh as a child tries to tie one for Elar. He points to me, and the others break into a cheer as I approach them.

"Master, I have been explaining to these noble men that you are a warrior from the Blue Mountains. They are kind. They nod and applaud everything I say. It was easier when the caravan leader was here with us. These men don't understand our language and—"

"Elar! Where are my clothes?"

"Oh, Master, do you not find these gowns comfortable? These men were kind enough to—"

"Elar! My clothes, where are they?"

The men go quiet and stare at us.

"Master, your clothes were quite dirty, so I—"

"So, you what?"

"So, I scrub… scrubbed them with sand as the caravan leader suggested, and put them out behind our hut." He stammers, looking down at his feet. His face becomes small.

I rush back to the hut, and Elar follows closely. I find my clothes, take them inside the hut, throw them on the floor and fall to my knees.

"What are you looking for, Master?"

How can this be? There is nothing. Nothing. I search furiously, pressing on every part of my tunic. I tear it open and lift it piece by piece, inspecting it closely. And I feel it. A comforting warmth rises in my chest. I hold it in my fist and open it to show Elar.

A small golden key.

"What is that? Forgive me, Master. I could swear, Master. I checked everything before washing. This was not—"

"Oh, dear Elar, don't you know what this is?" I smile. "This is the key to our journey ahead. We passed the test!"

"MASTER!" Elar shrieks and throws his arms around me.

"Enough, you little elf. We must return to our hosts. And Elar, get me something to eat. I am starving." I put my arm around him as we walk back to the courtyard. I had not noticed how silly he looks in his gown. And that ridiculous turban of his, fluttering in the wind.

Elar

I wake up early, as always. Father used to say a good servant is one who rises early and goes to sleep late. Outside, it is quiet. I bring my clothes in, arrange them, sweep the room and clean Master's sandals. If he hadn't torn his tunic apart, he would have had a fresh one in reserve. I have not seen him sleep before. I fell asleep at Mr. Fligroin's house, and in the forest and then at the lake. He was always awake, and I was always sleeping. I am sorry, Father. A good servant would not sleep while his master is awake. But no, he did sleep in the desert and I was the one who woke him up. That time was scary. What if he hadn't woken up? Also, he slept on the camel. Actually, all the times that I fell asleep were unusual, and today I have risen before him, so don't worry, Father.

Some of the skin on Master's neck is shrivelled. I saw it at the lake as well, when he disrobed to enter the water. His whole back appeared burnt, severely scarred and darkened. My skin crawls thinking about it. I better move away from him. I am sure he would not like to wake up with me looking down at his face. Not again. I pray that he never needs to. It was scary. So scary.

I quietly leave the hut and join a few men who are making their way to a place near the courtyard. There is a long queue of men outside a dome-shaped hut, carrying sand in one hand and a few small flowers in the other. The caravan leader is amongst them. He is almost unrecognisable without that ring between his nose and those large earrings that were dangling from his ears. No wonder the men have ear lobes so loose and overstretched, with holes so big. The ornament from his neck is missing too. He must be happy to have it off. I wonder how he breathes with it on. Maybe he wears it so that nobody can strangle him to death. Perhaps we should get one for Mr. Fligroin too.

The caravan leader greets me with a kind smile. "Will all these men bathe together?" I ask anxiously. I will certainly not take off my clothes in front of them.

"Our community cannot waste water. It is a sin," he replies in a tone that indicates I should have known. Thank you, Mother! That means no disrobing in front of strange desert men. "The gowns we wear allow sand to enter, which gently rubs our bodies. Keeping us clean."

Of course. The wheat fields. The sand. The endless itch.

"You must join us," he says, and asks a young boy passing by to hand me a bunch of dark blue flowers with a pleasing fragrance.

I take a fistful of sand from the ground and wait, trying to understand what the other men are saying to each other. Singing echoes from the dome, but it is not very melodious. Soon enough, it is my turn. When I enter, my fears are realised. They are all naked. The dome is open to the sky, and it is hot. Very hot.

"Throw the sand into the air," the caravan leader says while taking off his gown. "Rub the flowers between your palms and apply the juice all over your body. Although it might be sticky at first, it will cleanse you, and the fragrance will linger on and keep you protected from all evil. And, of course, it will help you sleep better!" He winks.

I try to look away from him, but there are naked men all around. I decide to get it over with and quickly disrobe.

"This ritual reminds us that we can be truly cleansed only when we are one with everything around us," he says. I wonder why he chooses to talk to me when we are both naked. I try to distract myself by joining in the singing, but unfriendly stares inspect every inch of me, preventing any sound from leaving my mouth. I finish bathing as fast as I can and quickly put on my gown. I don't bother with the turban and hurry back to our hut before I can be dragged into any more of their disturbing rituals.

*

"Master! The villagers are mad. No matter what anyone says, do not go into that dome." He is awake now, looking out the window towards the neighbouring hut. "The sand is in my hair. My head is almost burnt. The flowers smell nice, but they are sticky, and the villagers stare at—" I stop myself from saying more. I stand beside him and look outside. What is he staring at?

After a while, I manage to coax Master to come along with me to the courtyard. Meals are only served there. It is another of their customs, but an enjoyable one. The men of this small, close-knit community eat together while discussing various topics. It is a large covered area with a roof woven out of ropes, held up by wooden logs at the corners. The rope crisscrosses to form a web with very little gaps in between. It does a fair job of blocking out the sun, but last night, the gaps in the weaving allowed me to enjoy glimpses of the stars twinkling above. Patterned lamps hang from the ropes. When they were lit at night, they looked so magical. The light reflected through their intricate metal designs and stained glass created an enchanting atmosphere. It felt as though I was part of a unique celebration. Beautifully designed rugs adorn the floor. On top of each of these are neatly arranged sets of bedsteads, stools and low tables. A large hut close by houses the kitchen. Food is served in big copper platters with many small bowls in them. As I eat from mine, I feel like a prince. Their food is rich and spicy, I have never tasted anything like it before. There is so much variety! Spiced lamb, herbed rice, freshly baked bread, both sweet and savoury and different yoghurt and cheese preparations. For dessert, a special tea is served along with giant dates. Some men partake in a glass of camel's milk, as well. Master, who doesn't seem to enjoy anything, looks at me strangely while I gobble my food.

The caravan leader approaches us. He makes a strange nasal sound before speaking in his heavy accent. "Aaah, our guests. I hear you had a pleasant evening. And that you, young man, particularly enjoy our food." He laughs loudly while patting my back, and I feel like my entire body is being shaken. "You must try the water of the desert," he says, pointing to a hole in the ground covered by dried leaves and bricks. "It is the sweetest water you will ever taste." He calls out to a young boy, who returns with a pot of it. "Don't finish it all. You don't find much of it around here." He laughs as he winks at me. "It has been long since people from another culture have been among us. Guests always bring so much excitement and joy. We would be honoured if you would remain in our village until your next journey."

"Thank you for your kindness, sir, but we must—"

I interrupt Master. "We will gladly accept your gracious invitation and stay… as long as we can," I say quickly. The caravan leader smiles and pats my back again, shaking my entire body.

I don't look at Master, but what is he thinking? Where will we go?

"Aaah." The caravan leader makes that sound again. "We are happy to hear that. I am embarking on a short journey now, but will be back this evening. Although my people do not speak your language, they will take good care of you. If there is anything I have learnt in my travels, it is that when hearts unite, words follow." He bows his head and waves as he departs.

"Master! We don't even know where we must go! If it was not for me, Master, we would not survive two days in this desert!" I put the last bit of the date into my mouth.

Master looks at me and smiles. Why is he smiling? Did I say too much? Elar, he is your master, not your friend. Do you want a new master? No. No. Master would not…

"We must use the key, Elar. We must unlock…" Master speaks softly, looking at me.

"Unlock what, Master? How will we find what to unlock with that tiny key in this vast desert?"

"The box, Elar," Master sighs.

"Oh yes, the box. The box. Master, we must unlock the box. If not for me, we wouldn't have found Mr. Fligroin, who…."

I pick up another date and run to catch Master, who has already begun strolling back to our hut.

*

I spread the mat on the floor carefully, then Master gently places the bag on it. I feel excited and a little scared. What is in the box? Where will we go next? Was Mr. Fligroin right? I hope there will be more mermaids. But the dragon? What if he's too strong? No. No. Master will handle him. "Master, are you sure we should open this box? It belongs to someone else."

"The snake said that this is the key to our journey ahead… we must open the box." He mumbles and carefully takes the box from its velvet cover.

It is breath-taking. I am overcome by a soothing calmness as I look at the golden hue emitted from the emblem.

Master's hands are trembling. He fumbles with the tiny key.

I clasp my hands.

He puts the key into the lock.

I cannot contain my smile.

The box does not open.

Master removes the key and tries again.

Still, it does not open.

Master lifts the box and turns it around, looking for something.

No. No. No.

"The key obviously isn't for this box," I say, my heart sinking.

"It can't be," he replies. "Fligroin, the symbol, the snake, that realm... the answer has to be here." He mutters under his breath, carefully examining the box.

I try to take it from Master, but he resists. He closes his eyes.

"Please, if you can hear me... help me," he whispers.

After a few moments of silence, a gentle sparkle enters each of the precious stones.

"Master! Look!"

He opens his eyes and slowly inserts the key again.

A clinking sound. Then a cool breeze whizzes throughout the room filling the air with the fresh scent of jasmine. The box is open.

We are silent.

My mind is quiet. But is it? Then who is saying it's quiet? "I didn't know you could... Why didn't you do it before?"

"She told me, she told me, but I forgot that someone was listening," Master says, as if to himself.

She? "Master! What is inside? Open it, Master!"

He opens the box. And inside, we find a book, A little black book with the same golden crest embellished on its cover.

Master opens it carefully. The book also emanates a soft golden hue which now reflects off Master's face. Each page is a thin leaf of parchment, pale cream in colour, framed with an intricate golden border that appears to be a doorway, beckoning us into its secret, enchanting world. At the centre of each page, golden symbols have been painted in artistic strokes. Master flips through the delicate pages eagerly.

"What does it say? Where do we go next, Master?"

"I don't know! It is written in a language I don't understand! Not one word! How am I to decipher this in the middle of the desert?" Master is looking through each page again and again.

"Maybe we can ask someone to help us," I suggest meekly.

"Have you lost your mind, Elar? You want to give this supposedly priceless object, which, incidentally, belongs to someone else, to complete strangers? I forbid it. I knew it was all lies."

"Master, think about it. You were given this box. Mr. Fligroin sent us to the lake where you fought some sort of battle and were given this key. Then we woke up in the desert! I am sure all we need to do is *see the meaning.*"

"What did you say?" Master looks astonished.

Did I make a mistake? Elar! He's not your friend but your master. Do you want to be on the streets? "Dear

Master, I meant that you got this box and then Mr. Fligroin—"

"Elar, the people here don't even speak our language."

"Master, we must wait for the caravan leader to return. Did you not hear what he said? 'When hearts unite, words will follow.' I am sure it means something."

"I have absolutely no idea what it means," Master says, scratching his head.

"Haven't I always been…" I decide not to complete the sentence.

For the remainder of the day, I am the centre of attention for the children. I think they like me because I am from a faraway land. A new toy, perhaps. They take turns tying the turban on my head, making sure to tighten it even more when I scream, and then they burst into squeals of laughter. I play with them, chasing them with my eyes blindfolded. They are most amused when I knock into a wall or trip over a stool. Running as fast as they can, they dodge me and babble with excitement. If I stop, even to catch my breath, they clamour over me. We frolic about with a clay ball, running, jumping, and diving into the sand to catch it. When I can play no more, I help some of the older children milk the goats. Despite the heat, it is good to spend a day without a care. My only regret is that with so much sweat dripping from my body, I will have to go into that horrible bath dome again.

When I return to the hut, I press Master's feet, which puts him to sleep. His muscles are so tight and strong, my hands hurt. He wakes up as the sun sets, and we make our way to the courtyard to wait for the caravan leader.

"Aaah, our guests. I hope you were well cared for today." He sits down to partake in his meal.

My hands begin to sweat. What if he doesn't know the language in the book? What if he cannot read it? How will we understand what it says? How will we find our way ahead?

"Thank you." Master smiles hastily. "You had said that when hearts unite, words will follow." Master shifts on his stool.

The caravan leader smiles proudly. "Yes, dear, it is the wisdom of our ancestors. No matter where you go, it is through our care and compassion that we connect to people. And when we do, understanding always finds a way."

"Please help me. I need to know what is written in this book."

The caravan leader gasps when he sees the box. He carefully takes the book and opens it. He says nothing, but his expression reflects wonder as he gently turns the pages. The glow from the book reflects off his face.

Master looks on. My legs tremble.

"Exquisite," the caravan leader says.

YES! He can read it! I smile widely, looking at Master.

"But these words look to be written in an ancient language. These symbols are used in religious texts. I am sorry, but I cannot read it."

Master lowers his head, and I feel something sinking within.

"But one in our community may be able to help you. The elder. He possesses knowledge of the religious texts and is our guide on all matters requiring the wisdom of interpretation."

"May we seek his counsel?" Master asks.

"He spends his days reciting the names of God and is available briefly, only at sunset. I will take you to him tomorrow."

Master nods.

"It is done then," the caravan leader says. "We will visit the elder tomorrow at sunset."

Andahar

See the meaning. What could it possibly imply? I walk behind Elar and the caravan leader who are engaged in a loud conversation. Despite the warm sand and dry air, the surroundings are not unpleasant. As the sun begins to descend, the blue sky is taken over by a deep orange hue. It has started becoming cooler. The elder's house sits atop a large dune at a short distance from the village.

As we reach the top of the dune, the skies have transformed into multiple shades of red with purple peeking through. The huge ball of crimson slowly starts to lower itself into the horizon beyond, burnishing the sands a deep gold. The house overlooks a small oasis with a date tree arching over it, and the vast expanse beyond. His dwelling seems modest, although it's made from stone rather than mud bricks. Just before the entrance to his hut stands a waist-high stone podium with a little opening at its centre where a clay lamp burns. The small green plant growing from the top of the podium must be the source of the fresh aroma that lingers in the air. Two bedsteads and a couple of stools arranged around a table comprise the seating outside. When we sit down, Elar and the caravan leader are finally quiet. The only sounds we hear are the shouts of children playing, carried by the breeze in the otherwise silent evening.

After what feels like eternity, the elder appears, and we stand to greet him. He wears a white turban, and a matching gown covers his frail body. The wrinkles and crevices on his face are partly hidden by a silvery beard that flows over his chest. His earlobes hang low, but he wears none of the ornaments favoured by the other men. He could be mistaken for any elderly man but for the extraordinary softness of his smile. In his right hand, he carries a string of brown beads, and chants something under his breath. As he walks towards us, he slowly rotates the string, bead by bead.

The caravan leader folds his hands and bows his head. Elar does the same, and I reluctantly follow. There is too much bowing in this village. He nods and gestures to us to be seated while placing the string of beads around his neck.

The caravan leader begins to speak. I know not what he tells him, for the elder's only reply is "aaah," the irritating nasal sound the village men are experts at making. He listens attentively, glancing at us every now and then.

After a time, the elder smiles at me and puts out his hand.

"Please hand the book to the elder. He will see if he can help you," the caravan leader says.

Elar and the caravan leader gasp in awe as I remove the box from its velvet cover. There is something about its glow that does not seem to get old. I rise gently to hand him the book.

The elder pauses and looks at me in disbelief, then closes his eyes and mutters under his breath. He opens the book.

"Aaah," he says once again and begins to slowly read aloud.

I wait for him to finish and then look to the caravan leader to interpret what he explains.

"This book will reveal to you seven great secrets of the universe," the caravan leader says slowly.

"Seven great secrets?"

"Yes, yes," the elder says with a thick accent and a wide smile, and the caravan leader laughs playfully at his attempt to speak our language.

"Would you like me to read the first secret?" the caravan leader translates the elder's question.

"Yes, please."

He begins.

POWER

Life is but a journey upon which you embark.
As you descend from your eternal home,
you are each given a boon: Choice.

This promise contains your power.

The elder runs his long fingers through his beard, seemingly deep in thought, then says something to the caravan leader.

"The elder says, this is the most useful gift of all."

Choice? A gift?

"Your journey can flow in any direction, depending on how you use this precious privilege."

My confusion must be visible, for the elder begins to offer an explanation. "Not only are you blessed with the power to create the life you seek, but this boon also empowers you with the ability to alter its course as you desire. Everything is based on the choices you make."

As the caravan leader translates his words, the elder mutters and gently closes the book.

I do not understand.

A few moments pass in silence before the elder says to the caravan leader. "Elder says, we are blessed to be given the secrets of the universe."

Is that all? What does this mean?

"Elder, would you be so kind as to read a little more?"

The elder smiles as the caravan leader translates my words.

"My dear one, no answer will remain hidden from he who is trying to *see the meaning*."

Him too? My heart stops beating.

"Trust that the universe will always give you what you need. And my child, wisdom is quite like food. No matter how exceptional it may be, if too much is consumed too fast, it will be rejected entirely. Ponder what you have heard for a few days. Only then may you return to me." The elder stands and gently touches our heads. A gesture of blessing, perhaps.

As we make our way back to the village, I hear nothing of what Elar and the caravan leader are saying, and when I reach our hut and turn around, Elar is not behind me. I am not even sure if I thanked the caravan leader.

I sit on my mat, feeling worse than I did before meeting the elder. Choice. What choice did I have? I never saw my father. Mother died when I was young. Ned-Har and I were orphans. We did what we could to take care of ourselves. And Narcia? Does it mean I should have— But how? It cannot be.

One by one, questions locked in the prison of my mind are released. Sleep evades me for much of the night. Once the sun is up, I busy myself in helping the village men with their construction work by lifting stones. I am eager to go back to the elder, but his instructions must be obeyed. I engross myself in the stones, hoping they will help me find a way out of the maze of my thoughts.

Choice. Could I have done things differently for Narcia?

How? How could I have known? No. I should have known.

What if I had known? What if I had convinced her? What if we had left earlier? What if I had succeeded in fighting the guards? What if she were still—

"Andaharrrr!"

A scream rescues me from the devil in my mind. I find Elar hanging by my arm, trying to hold me back while the caravan leader looks on in horror.

"Andahar, please! You must stop! They do not need any more!"

My hands are bloodied. The sharper stones must have torn through my skin.

"Master! Stop!" Elar screams.

"Oh, they don't need more? Alright." I throw the stone down. How long have I been lifting them, anyway?

"Andahar, I am sorry. Our men tried to tell you."

"I am fine." I smile, trying to ease the situation.

The caravan leader seems unconvinced. "Why don't you come to my house? My wife will prepare sweetmeats, and we can enjoy them together. It will help you to—"

"That would be nice," Elar cuts in hastily. He pours water over my hands, frowning and muttering something.

After resting and eating dinner, we walk to the caravan leader's house which is just beyond the courtyard. It is more lavish than the others, two levels high and built with stone. A ladder leans beside the entrance, which is lit by ornate lanterns that hang by the door. The caravan leader announces our arrival to his wife while welcoming us inside. I can tell by the length of her response that it is not the friendliest.

We enter a large room with rich silk rugs laid out on the floor. It is bordered by thick mattresses that are covered with densely embroidered fabric. Multicoloured cushions of varying shapes and sizes are placed upon them. Long carpets with scenes from the desert embroidered in gold and colourful thread decorate the walls. Strange. It is the first time I have seen carpets hanging on walls. Two flimsy-looking swords and an even more shaky-looking shield hang between them. Painted clay pots and glittering metal jars have been placed in insets in the wall. Tall, filigreed lamps burn in each corner of the room. In the centre sits a low, carved wooden table.

The caravan leader is unusually quiet. As we make ourselves comfortable, he forces a smile and rushes to the kitchen. We hear arguing. He is trying to speak softly, but his wife seems frantic. The poor man seems unable to tame the beast. His daughter peeks from behind a flight of stairs. Elar asks her to join us, but she doesn't move and continues to stare at me.

Finally, the caravan leader and his wife emerge from the kitchen. She wears a gown with sleeves that hang loosely to her elbows. It is so heavily patterned, I cannot tell if it is blue or purple. Just the kind of complication a woman would admire. Her oiled hair is tied back in a single plait, and her tanned face is marked by freckles on the cheeks and forehead. A little golden ring in her nose and thick metal bracelets on each of her wrists are her only adornments, many fewer than her husband's. She greets us by folding her hands for a moment, then rushes back to the kitchen, while the caravan leader sits with us and offers a pipe, which I gladly accept.

"Did you gentlemen enjoy your meeting with the elder?" he asks, seemingly distracted. Nervous perhaps, quite unlike his usual self. After all, no matter how powerfully the lion roars in the jungle, he is but a mouse in his own house.

"I think that he is a—" Elar begins sharing his thoughts rather excitedly.

"I apologise, gentlemen," the caravan leader interjects. "My wife… The sweetmeats have not turned out well, and she is upset. It is the first time you have come to our house and she would have liked them to be perfect." He shakes his head.

I break into a smile. It's a nice feeling, as though something, somewhere, has opened up. For just a moment, an escape.

"Please, tell her not to be upset."

Elar jumps up and heads to the kitchen. The caravan leader looks at me aghast and runs after him. Where is this boy going?

A loud shriek. I rush to the kitchen to find the caravan leader's wife in the corner, pointing a knife at Elar, who is peering over the sweetmeats under preparation. "Do you have goat's milk?" he asks the caravan leader's wife, only to be met by a look of horror.

The caravan leader looks at me with eyes wide open. Confused. The poor man must choose between saving his life or his honour. Denying Elar is not good for his honour, but denying his wife, well…

"Could I please have some goat's milk?" Elar repeats. The caravan leader fumbles and asks his wife for the milk. She says something, pointing to a cup with the knife.

"Elar, I don't think—"

"One moment, Master. Some honey, please."

The wife passes jar after jar to her husband, who hands them to Elar, meeting his demands one by one. After a short while, he begins mixing the pudding. For the first time, I see a look of deep concentration on his face. He tastes it. "Hmm." He takes the ladle to the caravan leader's wife, who is almost atop the counter. "Please, try it now."

The caravan leader yells something at her and she puts the knife down. "I am sorry, Elar. She has never seen an unknown gentleman in her kitchen." He lets out a forced chuckle.

She hesitatingly takes a little on her finger and tastes it, then shrieks and laughs and begins babbling to Elar, who smiles as if he understands every word.

"She says she has never had such a delicious pudding before and asks how you thought of the— that is enough for now," the caravan leader cuts short his translation and smiles in relief. Both his honour and his life are safe. "Now she wants us out of the kitchen," he laughs.

We leave the kitchen and go back into the main hall, shortly joined by the caravan leader's wife, his daughter, and the pudding, which is served in small silver bowls. It is one of the better ones I have tasted. Elar is showered with enough praise to make up for a lifetime without appreciation. The caravan leader's wife rambles on to him about food, flavours, and ways of making different puddings. I am not sure whether he knows what he is saying or simply rattles back. Finally, the caravan leader gets bored with their conversation and begins to tell us tales of his travels, which are not very exciting, either. Elar, too, shares stories of his days with the merchant. The caravan leader's wife appears horrified. She weeps and uses animated words from time to time while covering her daughter's ears. When Elar tells an exaggerated version of the day I rescued him, they all break into an unnecessarily emotional smile.

"What about you, Andahar?" the caravan leader asks, "tell us about some of your battles. I have heard from young Elar that you are a famed warrior."

"I am no warrior," I say bluntly, smoking the pipe.

Silence. The caravan leader looks at Elar.

"Umm, Master means he cannot talk about his battles in front of the little girl."

"Aaah, I understand," the caravan leader says, trying to avoid awkwardness. "But I can tell you of my battles."

"You fought battles, too?" Elar asks.

"Every day I come home and get into a battle, young man!" he says, patting Elar's back rather vigorously, and they break into uncontrollable laughter.

"Thankfully, the swords are too heavy for her to lift." He points to the toy-like weapons on the wall.

He obviously must not have translated this correctly to his wife who is still smiling.

The light-hearted visit continues into the night. Most of the conversation is between the caravan leader's wife and Elar, the caravan leader playing the intermediary and adding his own opinions from time to time. It is relaxing, until it makes me think of what could have been.

Ned-Har

Although he rarely spoke and did not want to see much of me, his presence was a comfort. At least, he was close by, and I could watch over him.

I look at the bundle of letters that have been lying on my desk since his departure. It is always hard to come back to reality after experiencing the past through them. A dangerous feeling, not wanting to come back, wanting to live in the world of these letters. Just this once, I won't stop myself. I need it.

I undo the string holding them together. It is easy to tell which letters were written by me and which by Andahar. The warrior had just about managed to keep them from falling apart. If not for Narcia, I don't think they would be in one place. I remember as if it were yesterday. She tried to strike an agreement with me: I would give her all the letters in which he mentioned her, if she would board the ship. I teased her, saying it was against the code of brothers and that we could not wager over honour. We finally agreed that the three of us would read the letters together, and that until then, I would keep them safe. Little did I know, it was not to be.

I open the first letter, nervous and excited to steal some time with those memories again.

Dear brother,

I received a letter from Rolanha informing me that you were gravely injured, your heart almost pierced in the battle of Latnov.

I am worried for your health. You are all I have, dear brother. I think of the time when my knee was shattered, and I spent weeks in bed. You fed me, bathed me and told me stories of our mountains. Now when I think of them, I realise that the stories were rather poor, but I wish I could do the same for you, brother.

I pray to the Gods that you are well.

Lovingly,

Your brother,

Ned-Har

My brother Ned-Har,

The last battle left me injured, but not gravely. You know your brother. My sword is still the bloodiest. We captured the lands of Latnov, and the king is extremely pleased with the spoils. I could not enjoy them, though. It seems I will not return to my troops for some time.

You are brave, dear brother. I cannot imagine never being able to walk properly again. You did well.

Those days in the Blue Mountains... it sometimes crosses my mind to go back to our village. But then, there's nothing really pulling us, is there?

I spend most of my time lying in bed, but other than being obliged to eat terrible lamb soup, I am not suffering unduly. The physician has a niece, I know not her name... yet. She has soft, light brown eyes. It is the twinkle in them that is so unique. I think she knows my reputation, for she will not tell me her name, although I am certain I have seen her smile. She comes to my bedside every day, and somehow, brother, I look forward to the mornings when she tends to my wounds.

Don't you dare say anything about my stories again.

Andahar

How proud he was! Not a care in the world, boasting of the bloodiest sword even while lying in a physician's home. I smile to myself.

Dear brother,

I was so happy to receive your bird today. I am relieved to hear that you are healing well.

I know not if I was brave, but I am glad to have had you by my side in those dark days. For the longest time, I believed that my birth was a curse, as the village folk always said. After all, I exchanged lives with our mother to come into this world. Sometimes, I wonder how different life might have been had we found Father.

I have spent many private moments on this thought, and I must share with you what I now understand. I believe that my accident was a blessing, for I no longer had to chase the other boys in meaningless games through the village or participate in the horrid wrestling matches you loved. I could finally enjoy my time alone with nature. Most of all, by making me a cripple, life freed me of my duty to become a warrior. What a bad warrior I would have made! I would certainly have been taken in the very first battle.

I am sure your injury carries some meaning, too.

Please, Andahar, DO NOT, DO NOT, play tricks on the physician's niece. Unless you want him to poison you in your sleep.

Recover well and join me. I will take you to the most spectacular places you will ever see.

Ned-Har

How he hated my "sermons on life", as he used to call them. Alas! I had to try.

Dear Ned-Har,

I care not what people say. Your birth was a blessing for me. We were naïve young boys to believe that Father could be found. Now that I am a warrior myself, I can tell you that we have always been orphans.

Who knows how different life would have been if we had found him, or if we hadn't lost our mother? What matters is that despite everything, you travel the seas as a renowned merchant and I am the most feared warrior in all the lands.

No matter how beautiful these places may be, I will never board a ship!

As for the physician's niece, she will not fall for my tricks. She is not like the other girls and does not appear to be impressed by my strength or bravery, for she treats me like an ordinary man, and I don't much like it. After a lot of hard work, I have discovered that her name is Narcia. The kitchen boy here tells me that she was born in one of the southern villages of the Blue Mountains where her community grows medicinal herbs. The boy tells me that she is very intelligent. During her growing years, her uncle, the physician, excused her from helping her mother with picking herbs and made her his apprentice. When I try to find out a little more, he only tells me that she is often approached by suitors from within the kingdom and without. I wonder what he means. Sometimes I think she is playing with me. It frustrates me, but what am I to do?

She is beautiful. I already told you about her eyes. Her hair is golden brown. Whenever she enters the room, the air is filled with the scent of jasmine. She is like none of the women I have sported with. But it is not just her beauty, there is something about her manner. There is a playfulness she carries, along with a soothing calmness that touches my being. She seems strong-willed, yet gentle. As the days pass, dear brother, I think she is melting more than just my wound.

I have begun to walk, and soon enough I will leave the physician's house. The thought weighs on my heart.

More on this later, it is time for that horrid lamb soup.

Andahar

Dear Andahar,

I must tell you that your last letter surprised me. The warrior with the "bloodiest sword", the one who lives from battle to battle, returns to his troops with a heavy heart?

Narcia must have been sent by the Goddess of Love in response to all the times you mocked Her, taking revenge on behalf of all the women you abandoned at the break of dawn. Need I remind you that you and your 'oh, so noble' dearest friend, Rolanha, keep a tally of the women you bed? The one code you refuse to follow: "Respect women and treat them with honour."

Perhaps Narcia is the bearer of redemption! I am very happy, brother. The arrow that pierced your flesh has left you with a malady of the heart.

I look forward to your next letter.

Lovingly,

Ned-Har

Dear Ned-Har,

You seem to be enjoying my plight. As far as the code is concerned, I treated all those women with respect. I gave them the time of their lives! What could be more honourable?

I am now back to training, but it feels like something has changed. I go to the physician's house quite often. A good warrior must take care of his body, after all. So now, I get my every wound attended to by Narcia. And, of course, we also meet outside the physician's home. When I am to meet her, I feel great excitement, and when I am with her, I forget the world. Time just flies by. There is something magical about this girl. I am embarrassed to say that for the first time in my life, I failed to attend the training drills. She was curious about the herbs in the northern reaches of the Blue Mountains, so I took her to our village.

Oh, brother, I never noticed the beauty of that place until now. We walked up the mountain between the pine trees, which were still covered with snow. The air was clean and carried the scent of eucalyptus. The path was as untouched as ever, littered with fallen pinecones. The climb did not seem as steep, nor the wind as noisy as I remembered. We were alone, until we saw a white moose with enormous antlers. He was lifting his feet and stepping into the soft snow ever so gently, as though not wanting to disturb us. Once he realised we heard him, he stopped and turned to stare at us, his warm breath vaporising in the freezing air. It was a beautiful sight, brother. I was amazed that he did not flee when Narcia went to him and gently stroked his head. And dare you say "as expected", he fled as soon as I began walking towards them. What Narcia said after that was the sweetest thing I have ever heard. She said that maybe the moose could not see in me what she saw. Don't you dare laugh. I stood there thinking perhaps the moose saw me for who I am.

Soon enough, we got to the river. Brother, it was as cold as ever. I helped Narcia get across, but to my surprise, she was not perturbed by the cold. We saw a bear with her two cubs, reminding me of the days when you wanted to walk behind a bear and her cubs, imagining what it would feel like to be one of them. I told Narcia this, and she laughed heartily, saying she is eager to meet you because you must have a deep heart. I don't quite understand the connection.

She was excited to see our village. The houses were the same, the women just as busy. The place was unchanged, but somehow, it felt different. I was the only grown man there. Only boys too young to be inducted into the troops remained. The women warmly welcomed Narcia. She was surprised to learn that they managed the entire village. I never gave it the appreciation it deserves, but if you ponder over it, the women in our village do everything! From picking fruits, to tending to the cattle, cutting firewood, caring for the children, cooking and looking after the village's needs. It is truly impressive, don't you think? The women were amazed that someone from the South could cross the river and withstand the biting cold our village was avoided for. They happily took her around and showed her all the herbs, which she examined keenly.

I also took her to your favourite spot near the cliff, where the sunlight shines through between the two mountains. We sat there and enjoyed the slight but comforting warmth while eating berries. It was memorable, brother. I wish you could have been there.

After our visit to the village, Narcia seems closer to me. I think you would like her. She is much like you. She talks of mercy and goodness and believes that there is a God who listens to us all. She says that everything has a meaning and we have only to see it. Do you think so? I find it hard to believe. She talks of colours and beauty. She talks as if love is the only thing that matters, an idea I have spent a long time laughing at. I know not how but something inside me is changing.

She tells me she would like to travel the world. Although I did not tell her that I would never board a ship, I think you can help us with that. Perhaps you might take us to all those spectacular places you write about.

I do not want to, but I leave for battle soon and know not when I will return...

With affection,

Andahar

What can love not melt? What can love not beautify? What can love not transform? A warm feeling of comfort rises inside me as I open the next letter.

Dear Andahar,

I find it difficult to believe that place could be anything but dark, yet my heart fills with excitement when I think of the experiences you are having. Need I remind you that when I spoke of "meaning" you called them "sermons on life"?

I am only joking. She sounds like a delight. I will show Narcia the most beautiful places. It would have been lovely had you decided to join us, but, as I deeply care for you, I respect your decision to "NEVER board a ship."

The thought of you going to war unsettles me. Take care of yourself, now you have something precious to protect.

Your brother,

Ned-Har

Dear Ned-Har,

I apologise for not having written sooner. The battle was long, but I have finally returned to Narcia. I brought her a gift I thought she would like, a royal goat's head with the longest horns you could find across many kingdoms. She screamed when she saw it. I still don't understand why, but she was not too happy with the gift. Thankfully, she was happy to see me.

Oh, brother, I will be on the ship with you. There's no other way. She told me that she wants to marry me, and soon after, take a voyage together.

My heart fills with the thought of a tomorrow with her.

Andahar

A goats head! I laugh hysterically thinking of the time I first read that letter. Oh, Andahar!

Dear Andahar,

It has been so long. Oh, my dear brother. A goat's head? I know not what to say! I have heard from Rolanha that the whole kingdom says that the mighty Andahar is bent by the one ruled by her soul, Narcia. I also heard that Rolanha has overtaken your tally of women. I cannot say I am unhappy to learn that.

I am so delighted to learn that you two will marry. I will come to you soon.

With love,

Ned-Har

I reluctantly put down the last letter. I hardly recognise the man who wrote these. How different life might have been! We could have been a family, for the first time, but it all went up in flames. Tears roll down my face. I long for him and know not where he is. Fear gnaws at my chest. But no, the sage said it. This time must be different, this time has to be different. But I know not if he is safe. I sent him to battle a dragon. But life has a purpose, does it not? Nothing is meaningless. I must stay the course. The sun has to rise. No matter how harsh the winter, spring always comes next.

It must. It will.

Andahar

The caravan leader is interpreting for the elder once again.

"Before we begin today's reading, please ask any questions you may have."

"Thank you, Elder. In the passage you read earlier, we were told that choice is one of our greatest gifts. But during times of hardship, I have often felt that I had no choice."

The caravan leader translates my words to the elder who looks at me calmly for a moment, then closes his eyes and places his hand on the beads around his neck. After a brief silence, he replies. "Choosing suffering over healing is a choice that you are making."

His words feel like a blow. Rage engulfs my being. "How can you say that! You do not know what I have suffered!"

"Andahar! You cannot speak to our—" the caravan leader stands up in alarm, but the elder quietly nods, and he reluctantly sits down.

"Andahar, my child, perhaps if you were to accept your situation for what it is, you might find you have a choice?"

"I do not deserve a choice. Do you know what I did?" I try to control my voice, to subdue my bitterness. I close my eyes and try to stop my hands from trembling. Too much has been said.

Elar shifts in his seat.

The elder takes my hand. "I am aware that sometimes people make choices because they perceive that it was their best option at the given time. In all my years, I have not met a man who has made a choice he felt he was not compelled to, or could not justify, given his understanding, his evolution, his fears, his debilitating desires, his awareness or his place on his journey."

He pauses to sip his tea. "It is easy to judge another but difficult to ask what you would do if you were, not only in his position, but also in his body with his life experiences and his knowledge, evolution, fears, and complexes. If you possessed his every attribute, would you have made a different choice in the same situation? Think, dear child. You know the answer. Do not be so harsh on yourself. You are no immoral man. The choices you made were dictated by who you were, where you were, and above all, what you knew then. But today, you might be more aware, and therefore you can choose differently."

He looks into my eyes. I look away, hating myself for having no response. I don't want to agree with him. I say nothing.

"I, too, have a question," Elar says.

The elder nods.

"You mentioned a journey, a journey we embark on. What is that journey?"

"It is your journey to oneness. Your own path, which you have chosen to fulfil a deeper purpose in the grand scheme of cosmic happenings. Everyone is on one such journey of evolution, each with their own challenges, and their own lessons to learn."

The caravan leader pauses and looks at me. "Andahar, the elder wants you to know that it is true, sometimes the way things occur in life, it seems as though we have no control. However, your power lies in knowing that no matter what life places before you, it will never take away your ability to choose. Be conscious of the power this gift gives you. Choose wisely, for how you choose to respond to situations could very well be the difference between tremendous suffering and lasting joy."

I refuse to retreat from the battle in my mind. "Which is the best path?" I ask the elder, "What is the best choice?"

"No path is better than another, dear. The best path depends on what purpose you seek to fulfil."

His answer doesn't help. The trembling in my hands resumes.

"Similarly, there is nothing called the best choice. You must ask yourself what kind of a life you wish to live. If you seek a life of fulfilment, you might choose the path of goodness. If you seek a joyous union, you might choose understanding. The best choice will not be the same for you as it is for young Elar, who may seek something entirely different." The elder smiles playfully at the boy.

"Actually, Elder, I seek to be with—" Elar blurts out, but I gently squeeze his hand to silence him.

"And more important than the best choice is understanding that in this very moment, no matter what has already happened, you have the power to choose. In the very least, you have the ability to choose your words, your conduct, your actions. Even if you become conscious of it for the first time today and begin to make choices thoughtfully, you will soon notice how dramatically your life has changed. Use this boon knowingly, for it is truly never too late, dear child."

The elder mutters something, perhaps a prayer, before opening the book. "Aaah," he exclaims, then says something to the caravan leader. It frightens me when he makes that sound, as though whatever he says after that will stoke the fire waiting to engulf my mind.

"The elder says we will now read the second secret of the universe," the caravan leader translates.

FREEDOM

*Self-identity determines how the gift of choice is used,
thus the question, who are you?*

In the answer, you will find your freedom.

"Wait a minute. I am confused. Who is who?" Elar asks, momentarily pausing the assault on his nails.

The elder puts a hand on the young man's shoulder. "Who you believe you truly are will be the biggest factor when you make a choice, and this will greatly determine the life you live."

"Who I believe I am? I am a servant, Elar. To my master, Andahar," Elar cries out, seemingly dissatisfied with the answer.

"Since the beginning of time, scriptures and sacred stories have expounded one great truth: We are all reflections of the energy we refer to as God, and this energy is contained in every living being. Stated simply, we are the divine soul within a human body, the soul that has lived before this body and will live after it. The indestructible, the immortal. The true self. But do we have the awareness to see ourselves as the divine soul that cannot be destroyed, or do we see only the perishable body? Who you see when you look in the mirror will determine whether you choose to respond with loving kindness or cold insensitivity, whether you treat others with dignity or dishonour, whether you choose to give or to refuse another. The question is, can you transcend outward appearances? Can you look beyond the great illusion? These are the questions repeatedly asked across the scriptures."

He pauses while the caravan leader catches up with his words. "When you realise that it is you, a soul, merely experiencing that which you need and learning the lessons you seek in order to continue your journey of evolution, your choices will change. It is difficult to look at your life in this way, but all of us will achieve this realisation at some point on our journey. We will realise that we are all the same, differing only by how well we know ourselves. When you become truly aware of who you are, you will be free, my child."

"Wow!" Elar exclaims while I stare into the unending desert.

The elder begins to close the book. "Please, Elder, let us hear more today."

The elder smiles at me and nods. "We will now read the third secret of the universe."

PEACE

The universe is perfect, a flawless design.
If all that happens does not appear so,
there still remains a distance to be covered.

Walk ahead, and you will see perfection.
It is unavoidable.

This is the passage to peace.

I regret having asked him to continue. Whatever calm I had has vanished. "How can this be?" I ask. "People lose everything. They endure misery, suffering, the worst circumstances imaginable. There are so many wrongs in our world, so much pain. How can all this be perfect?"

"My child, the ways of the universe are mystical. Remember that your knowledge of reality is limited to what you know from your experience, from what you have seen in your present life, and naturally so. Our notions of what is just and unjust, what is right and wrong, good and bad, are all derived from what we have been told since we were children. Usually, these are not absolute truths but perceptions that may vary depending on whose eyes you see the world through. Don't judge a situation hastily. Accept that there may be aspects beyond your comprehension, that you may not yet entirely understand the workings of life. At times, life is extremely harsh and may bring unimaginable pain, but as you continue to walk ahead, all your questions will be answered."

He looks at us intently, running his fingers through his beard while the caravan leader translates.

"Look back on your own life, see the number of times situations that appeared to be great misfortunes actually played a tremendous role in taking you where you needed to be, showing you what you needed to see, teaching you the lessons you needed to learn. As for your question, Andahar, those shrouded in the darkness of ignorance may use the gift of choice for evil. Must we turn a blind eye? Certainly not. Such people must not only be stopped but also tried according to the laws of justice.

"However, if you have suffered misfortune without knowing why, you must still continue your journey with the faith that you are exactly where you are meant to be. There may be instances when you do not know what is best for you, but know that the universe does. Keep walking ahead, in the knowing that nothing happens without a reason. Even if things did not unfold the way you thought best, live in the awareness that the universe cannot make mistakes."

"But Elder," I shake my head, unable to find the right words.

"Dear one, I understand. The only thing you must remember is that if you do not see the perfection yet, you still have some distance to travel. Even if you do not believe it in this moment, you will discover it. This is a promise from God."

I cannot agree, but I hope what the elder has said is true. He begins to chant a prayer and closes the book.

Over the next few days, I look at myself in the mirror and ponder the elder's words. Could it be true? Am I a soul on a journey beyond my comprehension? Is it true that all that has happened in my life has been perfect? It cannot be! Our growing years, the difficulties we faced and what of Narcia? Will I one day see the perfection in that too? A wave of guilt lashes through me as the thought scurries across my mind.

"Master, tonight you must join me on the rooftop," Elar says. "The caravan leader told me we will have one of the most amazing sights." He keeps insisting, all the way back from our meal.

"Elar, I am tired—"

"No Master, please." He continues to pester me until I agree to join him for a few minutes. We climb the ladder to the rooftop, which is not much higher than the door. The endless sand appears tinged with silver, reflecting a gigantic moon that seems much closer than usual. I lie down and close my eyes to enjoy the cool air.

"Do you think that everything that has happened in your life has been perfect, Elar?"

"Master? Me?" He peers at me. "I cannot say that everything is perfect, but sometimes I get a glimpse of what the elder means. If my old master hadn't hurt me the day I met you in Corcusia, how would you have noticed me? How would I ever leave his service? How would I ever find an elder bro— I mean, a new master." His cheeks turn red. "If he was loving and caring, would I be in this desert, learning the secrets of the universe? I spent a lot of time wishing the merchant treated me well and asking God why he had given me such a hard life, but as I walked ahead… It is much like the game of puzzles I played with my mother. You keep putting the pieces together, and with time, it all falls into place. And Master! So long as it doesn't, you know you have some more to go!" he beams with confidence.

I feel lighter hearing young Elar's interpretation. A game of puzzles, but quite a terrible one. I look at the moon, a question swimming through my mind: Is this the meaning you wanted me to see?

Elar

REDEMPTION

Pain is an event which cannot be avoided.
Suffering is a process which can.

The light of awareness offers protection against
the darkness of suffering.

This understanding guides you to redemption.

After reading the fourth secret, the elder puts down the book and looks up at us. I love his explanations. Perhaps more than the secrets.

"Pain is an inevitable part of life. At some point on the journey, it knocks at everyone's door. Not a single man across the worlds has experienced a life free of pain or loss." He looks towards Master. "And I accept that for the person undergoing it, the pain is real and can be heart-wrenching. But remember, pain that is suppressed turns to suffering."

He sips the desert tea, which has a special aroma. I wonder what he adds to it. I shudder to think of Master's reaction, if I were to ask for a taste. I must concentrate. So, pain becomes suffering. Why does the elder pause so long?

"Suffering, unlike pain, is not an event, but a state of mind. It is a constant state of being that eats you from within and is strong enough to fell the mightiest among us."

Why does it sound as though he is always talking to Master?

Master interrupts. "But it is everywhere, Elder! How can it possibly be avoided?"

"Perspective. It is the way you perceive things, more than anything else, that causes happiness or sadness in one's life. Your perspective could very well be the difference between a life of joy and a life of sorrow. It is the one aspect in your control. Use the gift of choice to change your perspective on the situation, for it may not be as it appears. Use the gift of choice to understand the cause of your suffering and see the situation in a more complete way. Use the gift of choice to allow yourself to heal and to decide to move ahead on your journey. This is not easy, my dear one, but when you do take this step, nature will ensure that help is provided." He pauses, again. "Besides, what benefit lies in allowing perpetual sadness to become your permanent experience?"

He is even looking at Master now. What about me?

"Accept that like the seasons, pain will come and go. Wise is he who recognises the overactive mind as the harbinger of suffering. Often, the time spent ruminating over an event causes more pain than the event itself. It is this constant thinking, complaining, blaming and the meaning one assigns to an occurrence that is the real source of misery."

The caravan leader completes translating the elder's explanation. I hope he interprets it correctly, because I am a little confused now. I ask, "So, what must I do, Elder?"

The elder laughs. Why does he laugh whenever I ask a question? Is that the way to reward the most earnest student?

"Ask yourself, can you look at things differently? If your happiness is dictated by your perspective, why hold on to one that only brings you misery? This is a choice you must make for yourself."

A few moments pass in silence. I finally understand what the elder means! I look to Master and the caravan leader who are gazing into the distance. Are they still confused? Does that mean I am the brightest student? I smile widely.

"We will now read the fifth secret." The caravan leader announces, as though he is proclaiming the arrival of a king.

"Beautiful. The fifth secret will help you to better understand the previous one," he says, translating the elder's words.

HEALING

Surrender, and you will mend that which is broken.
Do not differentiate between the beaten heart and
the shattered bone.

In this remedy, will healing be found.

"I am so confused." I laugh helplessly, only to be met by glares from Master and the caravan leader, one with and one without a frown. The caravan leader does not even translate my words.

"Understand that healing is a process, that can neither be forced nor rushed. The first step in this process is accepting that you are hurt. Allow the emotions to flow. Allow your pain to be felt. Neither resist it, nor deny it. Do not turn away from it, for if you do, it will only fester within and slowly infect your entire being. It will gain power over you and rule your every choice, confining you to a never ending cycle of hardships. Have our ancestors not taught us the importance of mourning the death of a loved one? Through this act of mourning, of being vulnerable to the grief we feel, we open ourselves to the possibility of moving ahead. In the same way, we must acknowledge our pain, for by recognising its existence, we allow the natural process of healing to begin."

"Have you have ever shared your pain with anybody?" The elder raises his eyebrows. "If you have, you will know the feeling of relief it brings. As though a great weight has been lifted. As though it is no longer your problem alone. This is because in opening yourself, you have surrendered, and in this surrender, you have knowingly or unknowingly invited the universe to help you."

"With all due respect, Elder, how can I simply accept? How can I do nothing?" Master seems a little flustered.

The caravan leader hesitates but continues to translate as the elder nods at him.

"Acceptance cannot be likened to doing nothing, my child. When one is deeply hurt, it is the most arduous thing one can do. Society repeatedly misguides us. We are taught that emotions are a sign of weakness, that pain is felt only by the faint of heart. This creates a false sense of self that takes refuge in self-preservatory pride, which prevents us from accepting what it terms as defeat. It banishes us to a state of denial. Whereas, accepting the pain is an admission to yourself that there is hurt. It opens the casket of buried emotions. It lights up the darkness we are holding onto and reveals the root of our problems. Is this not what we would best like to avoid, fearing the discomfort it could put us through? Hence to acknowledge pain is an act of immense courage, without which, there can be no healing."

This is confusing.

"You may seek to change the thoughts or feelings that bring suffering, but there is a proper time and place for such an action. Emotions are not objects that can be replaced on an impulse. If we try to banish them too soon after the incident that caused them, or turn a blind eye to our anguish, we are only fooling ourselves. By denying their existence, we are only providing them a home within us. And once they live there, they are armed with the ability to attack us at any time.

"When we accept our feelings and understand their truth, we are protected by the armour of awareness. We may still feel pain, but with the increase in awareness, its ability to control us diminishes. It is only at this point that any action we take towards shifting our perspective will begin to work.

"Without acceptance, any act of resistance is mere denial, a form of slavery to the overactive mind. Healing can begin only after genuine acceptance has taken place, for how can one seek a solution without first accepting the problem?"

"And if I don't know how to?" Master asks.

"Surrender. Open yourself to the unfathomable powers of the universe. Have you not noticed that even when you do so involuntarily, miracles occur? Turn your face to the skies. Humbly ask for help, and surely, it will be provided."

I wonder why Master asks the question when he knows the answer. Does he not remember when we tried to open the box? I sometimes wonder what would have become of him had he had not found me in Corcusia, or had I agreed to leave with the mermaid. Master, oh, Master.

"Dear Elder, could you please provide insight on the second part of the secret?" the caravan leader translates the words he spoke to the elder.

Ah! He finally asks a question! I look at him with a wide smile but he only raises his eyebrows in response.

The elder turns to Master even though it was the caravan leader who asked the question, Andahar, Andahar, all the time.

"Mighty warrior, if you were injured in battle, would you leave a broken bone untended? Would you neglect a wound gushing blood?"

"No, Elder, most definitely not."

"Thank goodness!" The elder winks.

Finally! Someone who can have fun.

"External wounds left unattended *could* rob you of your life. Why then leave the inner ones, without offering them treatment? Don't you see that they *will* rob you of your joy? And tell me, my friends, what is the value of a life without joy?" The elder gently shoots another arrow aimed directly at, well, we all know whom.

"IT HAS NO VALUE!" I answer before anyone else can.

The elder smiles at me, but as he is about to close the book, his expression changes. He closes his eyes and places his hand on the beads around his neck. "Aaaah," he says softly, lowering his head as if in obeisance. Then he speaks to the caravan leader.

"It is time." The caravan leader translates, while the elder looks on into the desert. "For the sixth secret of the universe, to be expounded." The hair on my arms stand as the elder begins to read.

DIVINITY

You have only one true enemy – pride

You have only one place to go – within

This realisation, is Divinity.

The caravan leader commences providing us with the elder's interpretation. "Men fight many battles. For land, for wealth, for power, for pride and even kill each other in the name of God. This secret explains that we must fight the internal war, not the external one. Destroy your pride, for it is the one true opponent keeping you from experiencing a treasure beyond your comprehension."

Thankfully, Master raises a question, "How can a man not fight to protect his honour, his land, his people?"

"That's a good question Andahar, highly expected from a blue-blooded warrior!" The elder pats Master on his shoulder. I give up. He loves Master the most.

The elder gets up from his seat and walks towards a copper vessel that lies beside the entrance of his home. He carefully lifts the lid and dips a small tumbler into it. Then he walks over to the stone podium and gently pours the water into the plant, bows before it and resumes his explanation.

"By virtue of being born in this world, it is your prime responsibility to fulfill your duties. Be they to your family, your kingdom or your people. Remember that it is in following the path of your duty, you will encounter all the lessons you need to learn.

"Travel across the lands and seas, mountains and deserts, if you so desire. But one day, you will find that the only journey worth taking is the journey within."

I am completely muddled.

"A seeker of the light goes about doing what she must, all the while knowing that the only place she has to go is within. She knows that for all the battles she wages externally, and all the desires she fulfills, she might happen upon the firefly. But it is only when she wins the internal battle will she realise the sun. Ask yourself, my dear children, are we not all seekers of the light?"

A few moments pass in silence.

"How does one go here, O Elder?" I ask, secretly hoping to be appreciated for my intelligent question.

"Before I answer that, I will attempt to explain the place we call within." The elder says.

"It is a place of peace, of stability, of strength, of creativity, clarity and wisdom. It is a place of love. It is a place that can be discovered best through experience. Vanquish your pride, little by little, and you will begin to glimpse the world within where you will taste a happiness unlike any you have ever known. This, my child, is the one duty you have, to yourself.

"Many roads lead to this place. A mother can go within while lovingly embracing her child. An earnest student might travel there in the company of his teacher. A storyteller may find the road in his writings. A man partaking in sport could find his special place there. Visiting a serene locale amidst nature could transport you there, as could the embrace of your lover. Meditating or chanting the names of God are rather direct ways to take you there too. But be assured, no matter who you are or where you come from, you can certainly reach this place.

"You must find the activity that opens your heart and engage in it regularly. It will help in bringing you to this space of awareness, balance and strength. When you reach this place of clarity, and only then, will you be able to use the gift of choice consciously. Till such time you will use it only as a reaction, upon being tossed about in the illusory sea of life."

"Preparing food," I say wistfully. "I learnt it from my mother. When I cook, I feel happy."

"Do that, young boy! And with all your heart. For it will give you a taste of the spiritual world in a way that no amount of preaching could. And if you are good at it, we could partake in some delicious meals too!"

The elder encourages me with a smile before closing his eyes in prayer, signalling the end of our lesson for the day.

*

Master has not spoken a word since we left the elder's house this evening. He seems disturbed. Deeply disturbed. I should ask him why, but I am afraid. He lies on his mat and I on mine. The lamp is still burning. He must be asleep… no, his eyes are open. I could ask him now, but he seems angry. I get up to look at him, but he shuts his eyes immediately.

I blow out the lamp. Something unsettling hovers in the room. I know he is awake, and he knows that I know, but we say nothing, and soon enough, we fall asleep.

"AAAARGH!"

I am jolted awake. As though hit by a bolt of lightning. I dart from my mat and stumble towards the lamp.

Master is on his knees, screaming. I run to him. His eyes are red, and a black so dark. What has he seen?

"AAAAARGH!"

He screams so loudly, I cannot think. He holds his neck as though trying to free it from something, trying hard to break loose. But I see nothing there. Tears roll down his cheeks.

A loud knocking on our door. Everything is happening too quickly. "MASTER! MASTER!" I hold him, try to shake him. His screams are so loud, I cannot bear to be close to him. In his attempt to free his neck, he throws me into a corner.

I rush towards him again. "MASTER!"

"AAAAAARGH!"

He looks up to the skies, as if crying the life from his body. I do not understand what he is saying. The knocking on our door continues. I can hear the caravan leader frantically calling my name.

I empty our pot of water on Master's head. He goes quiet. His eyes lose their darkness. He looks at me, breathing heavily as water drips down his face.

I rush to the door. The caravan leader stands outside with a few men behind him.

"Elar! What has happened? We were awoken by the sound of screaming," he tries to look into our hut.

"Nothing. I—I think Master had a bad dream." I stutter.

"Do you need my—" he tries to push the door open.

"No, we are fine. Please… I apologise." I shut the door and turn around. My heart pounds and my hands tremble. I slump onto the floor and lean against the door.

Master faces me.

"I… I am sorry, Elar." His voice is breaking.

My ears are ringing as they did when the merchant would beat me. I say nothing. I close my eyes. I try to breathe. It is the only way I know to escape this horrible feeling. A feeling like someone is choking me.

Master stays where he is, his face buried in his hands. I have never seen him this way.

"Master… what did you see?"

He does not move. He does not speak. His body begins shaking, and he is sobbing uncontrollably.

My heart is sinking. I make my way to him and put my hand on his shoulder.

"Master… what did you see?" I ask again softly.

He shrugs my hand away and closes his eyes. His lips quiver. "I am fine," he says with his eyes tightly shut. His body continues to tremble. He takes a deep breath and wipes his wet face.

"Master?"

He says nothing and turns to change his soaked gown.

"Master, please tell me."

"Elar, leave me alone."

"No, Master. I… I cannot leave you this way." I gather every ounce of my courage.

His daunting bare back glares at me.

"Master, please. Today you must tell me. What did you see?"

"Elar, I am warning you." He turns around while raising a finger towards me, a few tears roll down his face.

"Why is your back so scarred? Why did you leave the mountains? Why are you angry all the time? What are you running away from?"

"ELAR!"

My courage vanishes. I try to appear strong, but I fear my eyes betray me. "No, Master. You… you must… what did you see?" My voice shaking.

"You want answers to your questions? You want to know what I saw? So be it!" Master shouts at me. He lets out a deep sigh as he sits on his mat.

The flickering candle tells me what I know in my heart. His is a story I cannot bear to hear. But it is too late. The warrior has already unsheathed his sword.

Andahar

"I was tied down, my neck in shackles. As I looked up, I saw that the entire kingdom had gathered. But I was not the one to be executed. Two stakes had been prepared. The princess was tied to one and Narcia, the other. I went completely still, seeing her in the garments of one about to be burnt. I struggled to free myself, but heavy chains held me back. The princess was screaming, begging her father for her life. The queen was wailing, and for the first time in her life, she was held back by guards. The king addressed the crowd. He said that Narcia had been condemned to death for practicing witchcraft and the princess for participating in it, an act of treason. He said they would be burnt to death, for no one was above the throne.

"Narcia was looking at me. Her eyes were moist, but she was smiling. I was screaming, begging the king. After all, I was his best warrior. I had conquered territories, protected the kingdom and was ready to give my life in his service. In return, he was depriving me of everything. I begged him, but it did not matter. He did not listen even to his own wife. He said that I would be punished, too, but first I must watch Narcia burn. The priest signalled. The king gave the order, and the pyres were lit. The princess screamed as the flames engulfed her. The crowd watched in disbelief. Narcia was quiet. Her eyes never strayed from mine. As the flames began to rise, she nodded, as if to tell me she would be all right. Then she closed her eyes. I cried out with all my breath. The skies thundered in response. Rain poured from the heavens but failed to douse the fire of fear in the king's heart. I used all my strength and broke free from the chains but was knocked on my head almost immediately. I fell to the ground. My vision was blurred, but I could still see my life go up in flames. Then there was darkness."

My heart beats violently as I listen to Master.

"Narcia was my love, my life. She was taken from me because she was special."

Master turns his gaze to the wall.

"She was the niece of a physician widely respected, for his skill with medicinal herbs. Everyone in the kingdom was under his care, from peasants to the royal family. But he was no ordinary physician. It was much later I discovered that he was gifted with extraordinary powers of healing. He took a great liking to Narcia when she was a young girl and suspected that her exceptionally kind and loving nature hid something marvellous. She was excused from picking herbs with her mother, and instead learnt to use them medicinally, under his tutelage. As time went by, his intuition proved right. He discovered her unique abilities and expanded his teachings to help her harness the potential of her being. She was very fond of her learned uncle and became his apprentice, following his every instruction. The most important one was to never let anyone know of their healing powers. It had to be kept a secret, for it was well known that if word spread, they would be burnt at the stake. If there was one thing the king feared most, it was magic... The prophecy..." Master becomes silent.

"A prophecy?"

"A greater king has never been,
Who cannot be harmed by what is seen,
All glory and riches he will enjoy,
Until magic makes his blindness destroy.

"It was said that the king was but a young boy when his father met a powerful mystic during one of his conquests. He asked the mystic to foretell the fate of his kingdom which had been battered by years of bloody battle. He feared that he lacked the resources to continue much longer. The mystic told him that his death was imminent, but when his son came to the throne, the kingdom's fortunes would change. Enemies would be destroyed, riches would flow and the kingdom would enjoy glory like never before.

"All this came to pass. The king grew very powerful. His territories continued to increase until all but a few lands in all the Northern Mountains were under his rule.

"He did everything in his power to escape the prophecy. When he first ascended the throne, he frequently sent out the royal guard to far corners of the kingdom to find and destroy any trace of magic. As the years passed, the stories of magic became so scarce that it was believed it no longer existed. The king's power had grown so, the thought of his decline was inconceivable. He was believed to be invincible. The prophecy was regarded to have been a falsehood, and soon, it was forgotten."

"What of Narcia's abilities, Master?"

"I did not delve deeply into these matters, but it was true that her presence was so full of love, her company refreshed everyone she met. In my eyes, it was her kindness that drew all the people of the Blue Mountains to her. It was her compassion that earned her many friends, the princess among them."

Master looks down before continuing. "Everything changed when the princess was affected by an unknown ailment that attacked her skin. It became scaly and turned green. The physician and Narcia worked hard to cure her, trying all types of herbal concoctions which would improve her condition initially, but after a few days, her skin would become darker and darker. Nothing seemed to help. The poor princess's malady was the only thing anyone spoke of. How she had been the most attractive woman across the mountains and plains, and how she could not even leave her chambers anymore. How nobody would marry her as she was rumoured to be uglier than a reptile. They even said she was being punished for evil deeds committed in past lives and that she deserved to live out her miserable life alone.

"During this time, Narcia was deeply disturbed. No matter how much I tried to console her, she remained downhearted. The princess could no longer bear to look at herself and attempted to take her own life by consuming poison, but she survived. The poison not only burnt her insides, it made her skin even worse. Her condition was so poor, she was confined to her bed. Nothing eased her pain, and her cries were heard throughout the castle.

"This was too much for Narcia to bear. She broke the promise she had made to her uncle and began to heal the princess. In twenty-one days, the princess was on her feet, recovered not only from the effects of the poison but also from the pitiful skin disease. A feast was held in her honour, and she made an astonishing appearance, looking even more beautiful than she did before.

"I was concerned about the spectacular way the princess had recovered, but Narcia brushed me off, saying she had finally used the correct combination of herbs. Unfortunately, my fears came true. The princess's recovery amazed the entire kingdom. The king, although happy, grew suspicious. He could not stop himself from believing it must be the work of a powerful witch who had arrived to fulfil the prophecy.

Knowing that this was the right opportunity to break him, I suspect that some of the lords informed the king that Narcia was the powerful wizard who had cast a spell on his daughter, and would slowly but surely usurp his throne.

"It was the day when we gathered to choose a date for our wedding, the day we would exchange rings in a small ceremony at her house. Ned-Har was also present. Narcia looked like an angel. She wore a white tunic tied at her waist, holding one end of it in her hand while effortlessly balancing a crown of flowers on her head."

Master's eyes well up again.

"Little did I know that the games we played that day, would be our last, that laughter would vanish from our lives that day. The palace guards barged into the house and dragged us out. Narcia and the princess were burnt at the stake soon after."

I put my hand on his, wishing I had not heard this terrible story.

"What can I say about her? She was extraordinary. She saw the world differently, much like the elder does. She was the one who told me that I could to turn to God and that He would always help me."

"Master, how did you escape?"

"I was to be executed the next day. I awoke in a prison cell with a tiny window from which I could see the smoke from the pyres and the houses they burnt, curling into the sky. Dogs were barking wildly, as if in revolt against the king. How I wished they would tear him limb from limb! Only hours before, life had been teasing us with joy-filled dreams. Now, all that was left was her handkerchief. As I lay on the floor in shock, I heard footsteps approaching the cell.

"'Andahar,' someone whispered. I was too consumed by grief to look up. 'Andahar, it is I, Renolph,' the voice said. 'We must get you out of here.'

"I was sobbing violently.

"'Andahar, we do not have time. Rolanha has managed to free Ned-Har, and they await you outside. You must escape tonight or you will both be beheaded tomorrow.'

"Upon hearing those words, I was infused with determination. I would not allow the king to snatch another of my loved ones. Never. As I stood, I heard a sound. Footsteps echoed off the stone and the passage slowly lit up as the torch of the guards approached. When they saw Renolph, they charged, screaming that I was about to escape. The two guards were no match for us. I grabbed one and smashed his head into the wall, while Renolph quietly put the other one out.

"Renolph led the way as we hurried down to the dungeons and through the passages beneath the castle until we reached an exit. Ned-Har was mounted on a horse, and Rolanha held the reigns of another.

"I ran into Rolanha, taking him to the ground with me. I beat him, one blow after another. His nose was broken, and he bled profusely, but I did not stop. 'You were invited to the ceremony to celebrate my happiness!' I screamed. 'I took you for a brother! But you came with the guards and took Narcia to her death!'

"He did not fight back. Renolph and Ned-Har pulled me away. Rolanha tried to get up, but he could barely stand. One by one, the torches in the castle were lit as guards scurried in search of us.

"I screamed, 'Why did you not warn me, Rolanha? I could have taken her away!'

"'I… I did not know, Andahar.'

"'LIAR!'

"'As I was on my way to the ceremony, I was summoned to the castle. The king ordered me to bring you and Narcia to the square.'

"'And you agreed? I would die before doing that to you!' Renolph and Ned-Har tried to hold me back, but I shoved them away.

"'Andahar, you don't understand, the king had planned everything. It was about the prophecy, after all! Every road from the kingdom was blocked. A hundred guards surrounded Narcia's home—'

"'I would have fought a thousand!'

"'The king told me you would be executed for high treason tomorrow and I knew I had only tonight to save you.'

"He was trying hard to convince me. 'It was too late,' he said. 'Nothing could be done. If I refused him, I would have died in vain, and we would have no hope of saving you or Ned-Har. The king used me as a pawn to cause you more pain. I thought of somehow getting a message to you, but even forewarned, you would have been trapped. You would have died.'

"'THEN YOU SHOULD HAVE LET ME DIE!'

"Ned-Har screamed, 'Andahar! We must leave now!'

"'No, I will die here.' I sobbed into my hands.

"'Andahar,' he said, 'Narcia would want you to live!'

"I reluctantly rose to my feet, wiped my tears and mounted the horse. 'You must come with us,' I told Renolph and Rolanha.

"Rolanha shook his head. 'No, Andahar, leave now. We will stay back and distract the guards. You must get to the plains as soon as you can. Go now. Please!'

"Rolanha and Renolph were able to keep the guards long enough, and we escaped into the night."

"What happened to the king, Master?"

"It was several weeks later. By that time, we had sailed away. Ned-Har heard that after the execution of his daughter, the king locked himself in a room. It was said that he was so deeply haunted by her memories that he lost his mind. A week after the princess's death, he was found hanging by his neck." Master grits his teeth, "How many nights I spent wishing I had killed that monster."

"But Master, he executed his daughter to save his throne, and then killed himself?!"

"Many a time I have pondered that prophecy. It was not magic that caused his downfall, but his own blindness. His fears were so strong, he saw no reason. His inability to look beyond them ruined him as no enemy ever could. According to the prophecy, the king was one who could not be destroyed by anything visible, and truly so, what hid inside him, destroyed him."

A few moments pass in silence. Master looks at me directly now.

"Since Narcia's gruesome death, I have not passed a night in peace nor a day in joy. My only feelings are regret and guilt. I hate myself for not knowing what I should have known. I hate myself for failing to protect her. I could have taken her away. I could have prevented her from saving the princess. What use was it to be the bravest warrior? She was my angel and I could not protect her. All my conquests were for nothing, all my strength, a lie. When she lost her life, I lost my will to live. Twice, I poured on myself boiling water to burn away the so-called Crest of Valour that was etched onto my back when I was accepted into the Elite Guard. It was the most painful thing I had ever experienced, but not painful enough, not even close to what she must have felt. A physician told Ned-Har that another attempt would surely kill me, and he made me swear to burn my flesh no more.

"How many times I wished my brother would die, so that I could end my miserable life, as well. Ned-Har could not understand that I suffered less from burning my flesh, than from the memories I could never escape. When I hear the elder speak of the secrets, I feel it is Narcia speaking to me. She wants me to go to the Mountains of Templetron. She wishes for me to *see the meaning*." Master looks to the ceiling as his eyes well up. "But I am tired, Narcia… so very tired, and I seek only to hold you in my arms," he says softly as though beseeching her to appear before him.

I wish I did not, but now I understand the scars on his back and neck. "Sire, we will go to the Mountains of Templetron. We are close, I am sure." I hold Master's hand in mine.

"You are such a lucky man, Elar."

"Really Master?"

"I saw the look in your eyes when you spoke of learning to cook beside your mother. And how—"

"Master, do you know what would make you feel that way?

"My Narcia. How she stroked my hair, her jasmine scent, her loving embrace made me feel… apart from her, nothing."

"But if you were to meditate or recite the names of God as the elder suggested…" I try to remember all the things the elder spoke of.

"The names of the God who took her from me? Never."

"Perhaps if you were to meditate?"

"It cannot be the answer."

"Master, we must ask the elder. I am certain he will help. There must be a way, Master. We will find it."

Master lies down and turns away from me.

Elar

Several weeks have passed, but I have not recovered from hearing Master's story. Why has God treated him so harshly? His pain has been unimaginable.

I have been helping in the community kitchen, the only man permitted to enter. I do not think it would have been possible if the elder had not given the women explicit instructions. At first, they were afraid of me, but after the caravan leader's wife explained something to them, they began to look at me differently. I have been learning how they prepare their food. The sweetbreads and the savoury, and the various kinds of yoghurts which accompany them. The meat is grilled with cumin and mustard and dill, and at times with coriander or basil. Once, they also used the precious saffron the caravan leader brought back from his travels. Their meals usually conclude with large dates, which are plentiful here. On special occasions, rice pudding made from goat's milk is served.

At first, I observed in the kitchen and helped with the preparatory pastes. Once I gained an understanding of their tastes, I was permitted to participate in the cooking. When I cook, I am at peace, and time passes quickly. I love to ponder how a dish might be improved, which spices could be used, how the meat could be made softer, how pastes could be thickened to perfection. A few of my experiments were loved, especially the meat pies. Oh, the meat pies! I flavoured them with more spices than I have ever used before and presented them with herbed yoghurt. The village folk began asking for them every day.

It would be easy to think they would like anything cooked with a quantity of spices but that is not true. For they did not like the broth I made. They could not understand what it was and called it spicy water. As I began to master their tastes, I expanded my trials to sweetmeats, beginning with the puddings they are used to and then slowly moving to those with dates, then figs, and then pomegranates. They loved every one of them. They were truly amazed, as was I, to taste a dessert I created with only cheese. I also made bread stuffed with dates and pistachios, and a bread pudding flavoured with cinnamon and dusted with nuts. But it was the little balls of saffron rice dipped in honey that really surprised me. They were crunchy on the outside and soft within, melting the moment they were placed in the mouth. It is as if I am an artist, who cannot sleep because he is plagued with the inspiration of one masterpiece after another.

The women bring me more of the desert plants. They look at me as though I am a magician, challenging me to create a dish with one new ingredient after another—a prickly pear, a yellow cactus, a pink one. I use them in ways they never imagined, and each dish is a success. Now, not a day goes by when the meals finish with dates.

It gives me such joy to see the smiles that break out on their faces when they taste the food I prepare. Something about being appreciated, being noticed, pushes me to create even more delicious dishes. I have become a hero, not only amongst the women of the village, but also the men. Who would have thought? Me? A hero? But when I think about it, it becomes clear. The way to a man's heart may be through his stomach but the way to his wife's heart is through her kitchen! When I am not cooking, I am teaching the women to improve their skills, and they love me for it. None of this would have been possible without the caravan leader's wife, who makes sure he brings us all the new and exotic ingredients he finds on his travels.

The other night while we prepared dinner, they asked for my secret. They said that everyone has one. I thought long before I knew mine. It is to share love, for it is so nice to receive it and so easy to give. I feel so excited when I think that I have the power to make someone smile. With only a little effort in the kitchen, I can make someone forget their troubles. What an ability to have! I did not share my secret, of course. A hero would not be a hero if everyone knew his secret!

Wouldn't that make everyone the hero? I am certain the elder will disagree with me.

The day after Master told me his dreadful story, he visited the elder. Initially, he came back to the hut to sleep, but even that stopped once he was given permission to build a small dwelling near the oasis. He offered gold coins in exchange, but none of the villagers accepted them. He spends most of his time in his hut, meditating as the elder taught him. He does not speak much and asks to be left alone. But I deliver his meals, and on a few lucky days, he allows me to sit with him briefly. He asks me about the dishes I most like to cook. He appreciates me and tells me I am doing a good job. Once, he even told me that his favourite is the saffron rice dessert.

Something about him is strange. Something different. I do not know what it is.

I often go to the elder's house. Master's hut is visible from there, and sometimes in the evenings, I catch a glimpse of him. He spends that time preparing himself, training his body. It is chiselled now, even more muscular. I had never seen his hair tied back. It makes him look so striking. He looks fierce while cutting through the air with one of the swords from the caravan leader's house. It appears mighty dangerous in his hands. He lifts one of the bigger stones and holds it above his head while running endlessly across the sand. In the setting sun with his torso bare, how majestic he looks! No longer like an injured lion. His scarred back only makes him more fearsome. The women and children gather to watch him, but I do not let them stand around too long, and I remind myself not to, either. He must not be disturbed, for all his strength will be needed to battle the dragon at the gates of the Mountains of Templetron.

I wonder when we will embark on that journey. The elder tells me that Master meets him often and is meditating intensely to know the path ahead. I wonder how that will help, but I say nothing. The elder knows better. I am excited about the mighty battle to come. No dragon will be a match for my Master. I miss him, but, as the elder says, if we are to continue our journey, Master must find the missing pieces of the puzzle himself.

Does that mean we will have to go away from here? The thought suffocates me. But is that not why I am here? To move ahead? What of the happiness I feel here? No. We must go. We must continue the journey. I must not be afraid.

I must see how lucky I am. I no longer need to worry about being hurt. I have a roof over my head and a loving master. He is a little strange and a poor student, and he doesn't talk much, and he has so many rules! But if it was not for him, I would not have known freedom, the freedom that comes with feeling strong, with knowing that I am special, that I, too, can make someone smile. I am not just a servant. I can spread joy. The elder says that if one looks at the world differently, one might find reasons to be happy. I thank you, God, for giving me so many. I await our next lesson. I long to sit beside my dear Master. I long for the next step in our journey.

Andahar

Sometimes calmness washes over me. Clarity flickers on, though it is neither concrete nor lasting. I have been working so hard, following the elder's every instruction. Long hours of meditation. Silence. Some days are good, some futile. Some days I continue without food and persist even though my body aches. But what have I accomplished? I know no more about the Mountains of Templetron than I did when we were in Stonegis. Perhaps the elder is wrong. Perhaps all this is hogwash. Simply fooling oneself into believing things that are not real. But no, I must continue. I must see the meaning she wants me to, nothing ever came of giving up.

My mind oscillates between an ocean of calmness and a volcano spewing molten lava that burns all the quietude. I have eagerly awaited the day when the seventh secret would be expounded. Today is that day. Today I must discover the way ahead. I hurry to the elder's house.

Elar runs towards me, his arms stretched wide, then fumbles nervously and extends his hand, instead. I ignore that and put my arm around his shoulder.

"Master!" he says, brimming with joy. "I have been longing to… I mean, how are you?"

"I am happy to see you too, Elar." I smile at him as we walk towards the seating area.

I greet the caravan leader who is seated, waiting for the elder. He has become more a seeker than an interpreter. Excitement is in the air, as though we are about to witness something grand. We sit quietly, exchanging nervous smiles until the elder appears.

"Are you ready, my children? The seventh and final secret." He looks at us with pride.

We smile and nod, understanding without the need for translation.

The elder takes a seat, mutters his prayer, places his hand on the beads he wears, and opens the book.

MAGIC

Be present in the only place of importance: the present.

Here is where your magic resides.

"My magic!" Elar exclaims.

"Yes, my child. You will find immense bliss when you fully experience the present moment. As said by the wise, the past exists but in memory, the future, in imagination. What truly matters is the now. Throughout history, great things have been accomplished by those who learnt to access this magnificent moment. A great joy, an engrossing experience, and the gateway to your own magical place within lies in the quiet of the present moment. Why is it that the beautiful place we call "within" is accessed only when you are doing that in which you are fully engrossed? Or when your heart is truly open? Be it the writer, the teacher, the sculptor, the musician or the young food creator we have here?" He pauses. Elar looks at me, beaming. "Because you are completely in the now. You are truly alive in the present, the moment from which you can access the unseen. Time flies by when you are present in the now, and it is in this very moment that all the greatest ideas, the grandest inspirations, were ever delivered. We rob our lives of great wealth by constantly thinking of the future, pondering the outcome of what we are doing right now, asking the perpetual question: What will we do next? The next journey, the next desire, the next destination. This action removes us from the present. It disconnects us from the source of limitless potential and deprives us of the ability to experience our magic.

"Sexual experiences are a good example of this truth. Is it not true that whenever you allowed yourself to flow in the moment of making love to your partner, every touch, every glance, was magical? Did time not lose its meaning? Did you not feel the joy of becoming one in every pore of your being? When the act was completed, was the love you felt not magnified? Whereas, when one focusses only on the climax, the end result, the magic and the connection is lost to a rather mechanical encounter. This is the case in other experiences, as well."

"I agree," Elar utters, deeply engrossed.

"Oh, do you now, little elf?" I nudge him, and the caravan leader and I share a hearty laugh.

"Elder…" Elar whines, his arms folded across his chest.

"Alright, I am sorry!" I poke him, before the elder continues.

"Do that which helps you access the quiet of the present moment. In that silence, life will whisper all you need to hear."

The elder smiles and begins to recite his prayer. The end of the lesson? No! It cannot be! Elar and the caravan leader are happy. They bow and touch the elder's feet to receive his blessings. They say something to me, but I cannot hear them. I remain seated, deeply disappointed. No mention of my journey ahead? Why did I strive so hard? I should have known. This is all…

"Aaah, my warrior on the internal battlefield, you have a question for me." The elder interrupts my thoughts, as though trying to pull me out from the deep crevices of my war-ravaged mind. I lightly bow my head, but it is forced.

"Tell me, my son, what is on your mind today?"

"Elder, for several weeks, I have been meditating and preparing my body for the battle. Yes, I feel calmer, and perhaps there is a difference within me. But now, I believe I am ready to undertake the journey ahead. I had hoped that the seventh secret would show me the path, but—"

"You have done well, Andahar." The elder sits beside me while Elar and the caravan leader prostrate before the plant in the podium. "Believe in the process. Trust that, at the right moment, life will show you what you need to see. Do your part, the universe will do the rest. You may be only one strike away from gold. Why despair now?"

My twitching face betrays my irritation. His words do not console me. They anger me even more. "How long? How long must I—"?

"Aah, dear child. We need only that one moment, don't we?" The elder winks and offers me a few dates that do not make my evening any sweeter.

*

Despite my exhaustion and the great temptation to give up, over the next few days, I intensify my practice. I sleep even less and spend most of my time trying hard to listen to the silence, as the elder instructed.

Tonight, my mind is restless. I step out of my hut to take a short walk, a break I desperately need. The night sky is clear, and I stray towards the oasis. I can see in it the date palm swaying in the cool desert breeze. As I get closer to the water, my face is reflected beside the dancing leaves. The tree suddenly feels much closer, peering over my shoulder as though to console me. Millions of twinkling stars light up the desert sky, although the moon appears to be off duty tonight. All of them appear to have descended into the water as if joining the tree in looking over me. In a moment, the nearly still water reflects a star shooting across the sky, leaving a trail of silver dust. I sit on the sand to take in the sublime gathering. As I close my eyes, a gush of breeze gently caresses my face, bringing with it a faint scent of jasmine.

I open my eyes to find that I have been transported to a magnificent garden. The grass is lush and green. It feels extraordinarily soft under my bare feet. As I am about to step forward, I am greeted by two white birds. They swoon up into the sky, intertwine their golden wings and sing in each other's sweet embrace, spreading joy and love throughout the atmosphere. Trees line the edges of the garden. Tall, rising far into the sky, I cannot seem to see where they end. A few shorter, fuller ones, laden with luscious and alluring fruit form a separate row of their own just before the majestic others. There are apples and lychees, mangoes and oranges, bigger and brighter than I have ever laid my eyes on. An intoxicating scent. It must originate from the flowers that line the trees, in impeccably laid beds. On one side of the garden, the playful pinks mingle with the shy crimson while on the other are cheerful yellows teasing the royal blues. I have never seen such large blossoms. Their shade and colour appears to change, as I slowly walk on. Bees hum softly, and butterflies hover above my head. There is wonder in everything I see. What place is this? Where am I? I hear a deep heavenly tune, and my gaze falls on the entrance of a cave. The breeze flows into it and fills the air with a celestial melody, echoing from within. It is dark inside, but I peek in.

"Looking for someone?"

I jump up and turn to see that the voice belongs to a man wearing a saffron robe. A sage. He bends down and appears to be tending to the pink flowers. I cannot see his face clearly, but his presence is powerful. I could have sworn, he was not there a moment ago.

"Oh, I see you carry that which belongs to the King of Templetron," the sage says without turning towards me.

Perplexed, I look down and see that I am carrying the box.

"Yes, yes." I laugh nervously.

The sage does not respond but continues tending to the flowers.

"Please tell me how to find the Mountains of Templetron," I ask, hoping he will know.

He stops what he is doing, rises to his feet, and slowly walks ahead to what seems like the edge of the garden.

I scurry behind him like a doe who does not want to lose its mother. The sound of gushing water fills the air.

As we reach the edge, the water becomes louder. The sage stands a little ahead of me and gently waves his hand over the edge to the scene below.

For a moment, I forget to breathe. The view is stunning. I feel I am standing on top of the world, looking down on creation. Far below us, clouds hover over what seem to be snow-covered mountains in every direction. Everything the eye can see is white. Water gushes from an opening somewhere below where we stand and forms a huge waterfall, cascading an unfathomable depth to the mountaintops.

"Where did you think you were?" the sage asks casually, as he strolls back to the cave. He moves slowly but with a strength I have not seen before. I quickly follow.

He sits cross-legged just outside the cave. He is completely still until a brown cat emerges and curls up in his lap. He gestures for me to sit nearby, while he gently pets the cat. As I get closer to him, I notice his mesmerising scent. His head is shaved, and his glowing skin adds to the radiance that surrounds him. His eyes are soft and seem to know every secret there is to life. He wears two spots of powder on his forehead, one red, the other yellow. His presence is as soothing as it is powerful. What a handsome being he is!

"Thank you, Andahar," he says with a twinkle in his eye.

I do not understand how he knows my name or why he is thanking me. I shift a bit but continue to look at him. I feel extraordinarily calm. He appears to be younger than I.

"That's funny! But no, I assure you that's not the case," he laughs.

"Wait a minute… can you read my thoughts?"

"If you say so." He winks at me.

This is no ordinary man. My mind is completely still as I bow before him.

"That's very kind," he says, playing with me.

"But where is the dragon?" My confusion pulls me out of the daze. "Did the Ali of Prusse not fight the dragon for four nights before climbing the mountain?"

"Oh, you have been fighting the dragon for much longer than four days." He laughs, then whispers, "You nearly conceded defeat."

Did I miss something?

"Oh dear, you bothered the poor elder so much with all your questions. Do you really not know where the Mountains of Templetron are?"

I think hard. And suddenly, just like the moment when the caterpillar finally sheds its cocoon and takes its first flight as a butterfly, I am snapped out of a lifetime of slumber. My eyes widen. My skin tingles. My heart beats faster.

"WITHIN!" I cry.

"Precisely," he says with an unearthly elegance.

"But I don't remember... when did I fight the dragon?"

His eyebrows raised a little and a beatific smile on his lips, he looks at me with the love of a parent.

"Did you think you would have to slay a living dragon? Now, now, it couldn't be that easy, could it? The dragon that prevents you from finding the mountain within is the mightiest of them all. The dragon of doubt, a manifestation of your own darkness. Whether it emerges as the dragon or the caped being who tested you at the volcano, it is but the force of your own negativity. These are elements of the voice that keeps you from finding your magic. The voice that tells you to give up, the voice that says you do not deserve to be happy, the voice that does not allow you to believe you can find the greatest fortune that exists. This voice is your greatest adversary. While you defeated the caped being of evil at the volcano, you defeated the dragon of doubt at the oasis when you were totally immersed in the silence, in the present moment. In that moment, you experienced the bliss of nothingness. The nothingness you reached through surrender. The nothingness in which you will always find what you seek. The calm place of nothing, where no questions exist and there is no need for answers."

I look at him in awe.

"Narcia was an important part of your larger plan in the cosmic scheme of things. Her physical presence in your life, however brief, was partly in order to provide you the experience of love and togetherness but more to open your eyes to a world beyond what is visible. Her death triggered the immense pain that eventually led you where you always needed to be—here."

"The pain, oh Sage. The guilt, the thought that I might have saved her. The loneliness. The hatred."

"Understand that in the grand scheme of events, nothing happens without a reason. She is and always has been on her own journey. Her death was not your doing. Although she is not with you in body, your heart knows that she has not gone, that she has been with you all the while, in a way that is beyond explanation. Have you not smelt the jasmine?"

"I have felt her…"

"Narcia has been by your side, softly nudging you, protecting you, taking you where you need to be. Now, Andahar, the time has come to absorb the priceless lessons of your journey. The time has come… to forgive yourself. It is okay, my dear, we all fall.

Lovingly lift yourself, embrace yourself. Look in the mirror and know that a forgotten child hides in that grown body. Just because years have gone by and you are now an adult, it does not take away the fact that you may still be vulnerable. Because your body has grown, it does not mean you are free from the effects of emotions, of pain, of fear. Do not punish that child for feeling hurt. Be kind to that little Andahar within you. Tell him you love him. Tell him he is complete, free him from blame and the burdens you have placed on him. Show him the love you showed Narcia when she was with you and the universe will show you a life of wonder."

Tears flow down my face as I feel a heavy load lifted from my shoulders. The weight I have carried melts away, like dew in the morning sun.

"All your problems and pain exist only so you recognise and heal the wounds you carry deep within. Everything that occurs, is to take you closer to your awakening in one form or another. *See the meaning*—in leaving you physically, Narcia sent you on a journey to a place where you were finally able to access the beauty within you, the beauty that will always remain with you. Yes, it has been arduous, but just as mountains are created by dramatic shifts within the earth, it is often in moments of great helplessness, that one finally surrenders to something greater than oneself."

I feel the shackles that have bound me for so long— guilt, resentment, hatred—vanish.

"You are exactly where you need to be," the sage says lovingly.

"The perfection," I mumble.

I begin to feel love and empathy for little Andahar, the orphaned boy who did what he could all his life. His journey, his pain, his punishment—he has had enough. He does not need to go on in this way. I want to embrace him, allow him to live, set him free to fly, to laugh. That little child deserves it all.

"I forgive myself," I say softly as tears drop from my eyes. I release the harshest and most unreasonable burdens I have chosen to carry. I look down at my hands and see beauty. I feel calm, knowing that life will take care of me. The love Narcia gave me led me to the love within me. Now, I *see the meaning*. She took me to the world within. She gave me a companion I can never lose, sunlight that can never fade. I bow down to her. I thank her for coming into my life. I understand what she did for me. Now, I will give myself that love, the love she would want me to have. And what is there not to love? I carry the beautiful Mountains of Templetron within me. I release the past. I no longer need to cling to it.

"I am beautiful. I am whole." I feel magnificent as tears flow down my face, taking with them all that I had withheld, all that prevented me from healing. It leaves me feeling fresh, clean, and light.

I begin to laugh. I laugh and laugh and laugh.

"So, there really is no king to whom I must deliver this box?" I ask laughing, shaking my head.

"Oh, I think you know there is only one king here, and you have given him more than a book." The sage smiles widely.

Ned-Har, you little rascal. You knew it all along. A feeling of warmth rises in my chest.

"Will I at least be granted a wish?" I smile looking at the sage's divine face.

"Ah yes, that you will. Make your wish." He nods with a glint in his eye.

I close my eyes with a wide, wide smile.

Andahar

"Oh my God!" the elder exclaims upon seeing me. He drops the pot he was holding, treating the sand to a splash of camel's milk.

"Andahar! You… you went there!" He smiles in awe, his hands on his cheeks.

"I did, dear Elder," I reply, bowing before him.

"I have come to bid you farewell. Bless me, oh loving Elder. I seek to undertake a new journey."

He puts his hand on my head and chants a blessing, then embraces me. I am filled with gratitude for his kindness and grace.

I make my way back to the village, to the hut that became my home many months ago and begin to gather my belongings.

"Oh, look who has come home!" Elar charges through the door.

"Elar," I smile and open my arms.

"Wait… what did you do?" His eyes get smaller as he stares at me keenly.

I never thought a day would come when this boy would stop me in my tracks as I opened my arms to him. His eyes widen. He is trying to say something, but no words come.

"YOU DID IT!" he screams, his hands on his head.

"How observant you have become!" I tease him.

He runs to me, hugs me, then looks around the room suspiciously.

"What are you doing to the… Why are you collecting your things?"

"Elar, I must undertake one more journey."

"A journey? How? Where?"

"The caravan leader has been kind enough to give me a camel."

He goes quiet.

"You are going on a journey without me?" His unblinking gaze has lost all trace of excitement.

"Elar, brother, you are happy and have a life here. I will give you my gold coins so you will not need to serve anyone ever again. But I must go now. I must write the next chapter of my journey." I had not realised how difficult this would be.

"Master," he swallows. "I did not leave you for that mermaid. How can you think I will leave you now?"

"Mermaid?" I ask, surprised.

"I tried to tell you, Master. At the lake. After my eyes closed, the mermaid, the most beautiful one, transformed into a woman and led me through a meadow. Every time I tried to get close to her, she walked farther away. I was led into a house. It was in Corcusia. I saw myself a merchant, wearing a hat and shining robes. I was being served at a table. One of the servants was the merchant whom I used to serve! It felt good to see that." He pauses as I listen intently.

"With me at the table, sat the mermaid in her human form, adorned with jewels from head to toe. She held my hand as we looked at each other lovingly. I had everything I ever desired," he says dreamily. "The mermaid stood beside me watching this scene. She kept telling me how beautiful it all was, and that we only needed each other to make it come true. I was mesmerised. She kept asking me if I wanted that life, if I wanted her. I told her that I did. But then she said I would have to leave you, take the box and go with her. She said I had served long enough and received nothing in return. She told me I must decide quickly, as we had very little time. She begged me and said that if I left you, my destiny would change. Her voice grew louder and louder with each request, as she urged me to leave. In that moment, I knew I couldn't. I turned towards her and said in a calm voice that I would never leave you. Then she vanished. Everything went black. And I woke up in the desert."

That was his test! That is how he got across!

"My time here has taught me that my happiness is a state I can create no matter where I go. And you are the reason I learnt this. I would leave this place a hundred times over to be at your side."

I put my hand on his shoulder. The tears in my eyes reveal the secrets of my heart. He smiles gleefully, eagerly anticipating my next words.

"Elar, what I really wish to say is… You had better ask the caravan leader for another camel. I refuse to share mine with you." And I burst into a laugh.

"Oh, I don't want to share a camel with you," he grumbles, as I continue laughing.

*

As we walk towards the camels, we wave to the caravan leader and the teary-eyed villagers who have gathered to bid us farewell. I would never have imagined that it would turn out this way. The men applaud us while the women and children weep. They treat Elar as they would a hero, reaching their hands out to touch him and pat his back. They give him gifts of spices, sweets and flowers. He seems to greatly enjoy the show and imparts his final guidance on the recipe for the much-loved saffron honey dessert. After we mount the camels, he waves dramatically, blowing kisses to everyone gathered. A king would be jealous.

"Are you ready, or should we wait for the sun to set?" I ask.

"No, we may leave now." He gives his blessing.

"So, where do we go next!" he asks excitedly. "But wait, you did not tell me your wish!"

I roll my eyes.

"Master! Tell me! Did you wish for more wishes?"

"Oh! And will we meet the mermaids again?" His eyes light up.

"Or demons?"

"At least something for you to fight!"

"TELL ME WHAT YOU WISHED FOR!"

Here we go again. "Silence, Elar," I say with a smile. And we ride on into the desert.

≠≠≠≠≠

About the Author

After he graduated from the University of Exeter in the United Kingdom, Kabir returned to India and began working as a third-generation member in his family-owned enterprise. During the following years, despite being immersed in the corporate world, he continued his search for a deeper meaning in life, eventually deciding to move on and follow his inner calling.

Kabir can be reached at *thetranquiltiger1@gmail.com*

Made in the USA
Coppell, TX
06 January 2024

27363794R00125